NOTHING ELSE BUT MIRACLES

NOTHING ELSE BUT MIRACLES

Kate Albus

MARGARET FERGUSON BOOKS
HOLIDAY HOUSE · NEW YORK

Margaret Ferguson Books

Printed and bound in July 2023 at Maple Press, York, PA, USA.

www.holidayhouse.com

First Edition

1 3 5 7 9 10 8 6 4 2

Library of Congress Cataloging-in-Publication Data

Names: Albus, Kate, author.

Title: Nothing else but miracles / Kate Albus.

Description: First edition. | New York : Margaret Ferguson Books/
Holiday House, 2023. | Audience: Ages 9–12. | Audience: Grades 4–6.
Summary: "Living on their own on Manhattan's Lower East Side while their
Pop is off fighting in World War II, twelve-year-old Dory Byrne and her
brothers discover an abandoned hotel that proves a perfect hideout just
when they need it most"—Provided by publisher.
Identifiers: LCCN 2022040898 | ISBN 9780823451630 (hardcover)
Subjects: CYAC: Brothers and sisters—Fiction. | Hotels, motels, etc.—Fiction.
World War, 1939–1945—Fiction. | Lower East Side (New York, N.Y.)—Fiction.
Classification: LCC PZ7.1.A432 No 2023 | DDC [Fic]—dc23
LC record available at https://lccn.loc.gov/2022040898

ISBN: 978-0-8234-5163-0 (hardcover)

For my father, who told tales of old New York,
and my mother, who encouraged me
to write such things down.

NOTHING
ELSE BUT
MIRACLES

THE
GREEN
GODDESS

If you were looking for Dory Byrne—not that there's any reason you would be—you'd most likely find her at the Castle.

Which makes it sound as if this is a story about a princess.

It isn't.

Castle Clinton, as it was known to most people, wasn't actually a castle at all. It was—or had been—at various points in its history:

1. A fort
2. A restaurant and opera house
3. An immigration processing center
4. An aquarium
5. A ruin

Which is what it was now. An empty place, half-demolished. Derelict. Dangerous, even. But a place whose remaining ramparts, if you were a slightly underfed girl of twelve who wasn't afraid to climb over a little rubble, provided an excellent view of the Statue of Liberty.

So now you know.

The Castle, as it turns out, sits not on a verdant hill in the European countryside, but in a place called Battery Park, at the southern tip of the island of Manhattan.

New York City.

And Dory Byrne sits—well, sat—on the Castle wall.

It was April. It was starting to drizzle. And Dory's coat left a lot to be desired. A sensible child would have been indoors, sipping a cup of Ovaltine. Asking for help with her homework, maybe. But Dory Byrne prided herself on not being especially sensible. Also, there hadn't been any Ovaltine in her kitchen in some time, and homework wasn't on her mind at the moment, even if there had been an adult around to help with it.

Which there wasn't.

She looked out at the Statue of Liberty as she had done so many times since Pop went off to fight in the war. With the help of his binoculars, Dory could see her, plain as day.

"We need him back, Libby," she said. "Please look out for him. Please."

It was silly, Dory knew, to feel such connection to a copper giant. A French copper giant, for heaven's sake. But the way she figured, the Green Goddess had been the

2

last one to see Pop's navy ship go, and she'd be the first to see it return. With him on it. Safe and sound.

Dory pulled her threadbare coat a little tighter and waved goodbye to Libby. She got to her feet and scrambled down the pile of debris adjoining the ramparts. Home was eighteen or twenty blocks north, depending on how you went, and the wind off the East River flung wet needles at her bare neck, hurrying her footsteps.

At the corner of Fulton and Pearl, she saw Mrs. Schmidt mopping the day's accumulated grime from her bakery's stoop. Mrs. Schmidt waved her over, like always. Dory crossed diagonally and stepped around the bucket to follow her inside. The warmth of the place, ripe with yeast and butter, surrounded Dory like a blanket.

Mrs. Schmidt collected a waxed-paper sack from a shelf under the counter and began filling it with leftover crullers.

"You should be wearing a dress," she said, her German accent thick.

Dory didn't like to think about Mrs. Schmidt being German. Given where her father was. And who he was fighting. She cleared her throat. Trousers were more efficient.

"And where's your hat?" Mrs. Schmidt asked. "Have you got one?"

Dory nodded. Which was a lie, if nodding counted as a lie. Dory had given her hat to her kid brother, Pike. His had started unraveling last month, making it fairly useless as hats go.

"Well, put it on, child." Mrs. Schmidt handed over the crullers. "You'll catch your death and end up like your mama."

Dory clutched the sack in her right hand, balled her left so tightly her fingernails dug half-moons in her palms. "Yes, Mrs. Schmidt. And thank you."

She fled the bakery and walked back out into the pelting rain.

*

The Byrnes' apartment was one of six units above a ground-floor pharmacy. Two per floor, with a shared bathroom in the hall. It was a regular sort of apartment, as the Lower East Side went. A tiny kitchen and living room, combined, at the front. Two bedrooms in the back. Having two bedrooms made the Byrnes feel wealthy.

They were not. But it was nice, feeling that way.

The building entrance was on Catherine Street, but Dory always went around the corner to the Madison Street side and used the fire escape. The ladder past the ground floor had rusted in place long before her time, making the fire escape the most convenient entrance. It meant that she didn't have to remember a key. Or smell the funk of the stairwell. Besides which, climbing in the living room window was altogether more Dory Byrne's style.

Dusk loomed as she scrambled up the ladder past the pharmacy sign. The neon PRESCRIPTIONS arrow had been unlit for two years now, the whole city's glitter dimmed in case Hitler or his associates got it in their heads to attack.

She crept past Mrs. Kopek's second-floor window, hoping to avoid a lengthy chat about her neighbor's bunions.

Her pace quickened at the third-floor landing outside Mr. Kowalczyk's apartment. She knew he'd be sitting at his window, just like always, and that when he saw her he would look away, just like always. Mr. Kowalczyk was what Pop called a recluse. In all the years she'd lived in the Catherine Street building, Dory had never actually talked to him. Only passed him at his window like she did now, their eyes connecting for just a second before Dory continued up the stairs to her apartment.

She juddered the peeling window up its weathered track and stepped inside, landing nimbly by the living room sofa and depositing the bag of crullers on its arm.

"You forgot me!" Pike cried.

"What?" Dory looked first at Pike, seated at the wobbly kitchen table, then at her older brother, Fish, who stood next to him, glowering.

"You forgot him!" Fish shouted.

"I did not! You were supposed to pick him up!"

"I was not!"

"Were so, Fish!"

"Was not, Doris!"

Dory stamped her foot. "Don't call me that!"

Pike put his head down on the table and began to cry.

Fish took a deep breath. "Aw, Pike, cut that out." But even as he said the words, he was lifting Pike in his arms, letting his brother weep snotty tears into his neck. He looked at Dory. "You said you'd be responsible for him today, Dor."

"No I didn't!" Dory thought for a moment. "I—" She felt heat rise to her cheeks as she recalled that morning, remembered mumbling something *yes*-ish when Fish asked her if she'd collect Pike from the library. "Sorry, Pike." She looked at the floor. "How'd you get home?"

Fish shifted Pike to his other hip. "He walked. I found him here all alone."

Pike sometimes walked to the public library just across from PS 42 after school let out. His penchant for libraries worked to Dory's advantage, leaving her free to do as she pleased many afternoons, though she didn't understand why anybody would hang out in a library by choice. What she did understand was that, at only eight, Pike was too little to walk the nine blocks home alone.

"Oh." Dory approached her brothers and laid a tentative hand on Pike's back. He was hot from crying. She felt guilt flare, painful, somewhere behind her ribs. "I'm real sorry, Pike. Honest, I am. I'll never forget again."

Pike turned to scowl at her, leaving a trail of snot on the collar of Fish's shirt.

"It's the second time this month you've forgotten," Fish said.

"No it isn't!"

Fish only looked at her, disappointment oozing out of him, making him look older than his seventeen years. "You've gotta be more responsible, Dor."

The guilt in Dory's rib cage did a triple flip and landed as anger.

"This is all your fault anyhow, Fish! If Pop was still here, I wouldn't have to be responsible! If Pop was still here, neither one of us would have to be responsible!"

Fish closed his eyes for a long moment. When he spoke, his voice was low and conciliatory. "We would so, Dory. We both walked Pike home plenty of times before Pop left."

Which was true. But that didn't mean Dory was going to let Fish off the hook. "If you hadn't told Pop it was okay to go, then everything would still be the way it's supposed to be!"

Which was also true.

Sort of.

If we're being honest here.

✳

Pop had been called up five months ago, in November 1943. It was the second time he'd been told to go fight Hitler, the first being right after Pearl Harbor. He'd asked Uncle Sam for an exception back then, and when he opened the notice that November evening, his first instinct was to ask again. After all, Fish was newly seventeen, Dory was twelve, Pike was not quite eight, and Mama was dead. (You've probably worked that last part out by now, with what the bakery lady said about Dory catching her death and ending up like her mama. It was tuberculosis that took her. When Dory was six. And Mrs.

Schmidt didn't quite have her facts straight. Nobody ever got tuberculosis from not wearing a hat.)

Anyhow, Pop had been sitting there in the kitchen, the notice in front of him, his face grave, when Fish looked up from the game of Sorry! he was playing with Dory and Pike.

"What's the matter, Pop?"

Pop held up the paper, gave a small shake of his head. "Called up again."

Oblivious to everything but the game, Dory drew a Sorry card and grinned wide. She moved a blue pawn out of her Start, sending one of Fish's yellows back to his. "Sorry, Fish!"

(She wasn't. Not at all.)

But Fish hadn't even heard her. He rose from the floor and went to look over Pop's shoulder at the notice. Crossed his arms over his chest. "Navy," he read. "Just like last time."

One side of Pop's mouth twitched in a sort of wry, fleeting smile. "Like I always say, Byrnes are meant to be on the water."

For nearly twenty years, all the jobs Pop had done—and he'd done quite a few, trying to keep his family afloat, to use an appropriate phrase—were water jobs. Long-shoreman. Second mate on a trawler. Dock repairman.

When he and Cordelia had married, back in '27, they'd laughed about their nautical names (*Cordelia* means "daughter of the sea"; *Hurley*—Pop's name—means "ocean tide"). Cordelia had declared that their children would be similarly named for the sea. Hence:

8

1. Fisher (probably self-explanatory)
2. Doris (which means "gift of the ocean," though Dory didn't think *Doris* was much of a gift, name-wise)
3. Pike (a type of fish)

(To be fair, pike are freshwater fish, so the youngest Byrne wasn't technically named for the sea, but we can all agree that being called Pike is preferable to being called Yellowfin or Croaker.)

In any case.

Fish put a hand on his father's shoulder. "What are you gonna do, Pop?"

Pop started to say he was going to request another exception. But he didn't.

What he did was swallow a lump in his throat at the thought of all the friends and friends of friends who were already over there. Every able-bodied man from the neighborhood. Except Ivan Sidorov from the shoe store over on Delancey, and everybody called him a coward, right to his face. Even Mr. Tsitak from apartment 4, downstairs, was off fighting, his wife home with their six-month-old twins. More than half the men from the docks were gone. Crab Conklin and Sid Blau were both in the Mediterranean somewhere. Declan Murray went to Japan and got some sort of medal for bravery, and the day after the medal ceremony, Declan's mother went and joined the coast guard. The very next day. His mother, for Pete's sake.

All of them, doing right by their country. All of

them—how had President Roosevelt put it?—keeping "the floods of aggression and barbarism and wholesale murder from engulfing us all."

You might think it would be a relief, not having to face barbarism, but it left Pop with an empty feeling. It was quite a load to bear, the not going.

Which is why he didn't say anything about an exception. What he said instead was, "I'm thinking on it."

Dory looked up from the game, her face puckered.

Pop saw it, the puckering. "Every man's got to think on it, honey."

She swallowed hard. "Not every man who's a pop."

"Dory." Fish sighed. "Do you have any idea how many pops have already left?"

Dory had a very precise idea, in fact. If she pictured her classroom at PS 42 as a grid, the kids whose pops had gone off fighting included three from row one (Maeve Morrison, Vincent Morello, and Irving Abrams—Irving's pop was killed at Midway); two from row two (John Kelly and Joseph Ricci); one from row three (Susan Schneider— her pop died at Guadalcanal); and four from row four (Evie Sullivan, Ernest Klein, Corrinne Tompkins, and Ronald DeMarco, the new boy who picked his nose when he thought nobody was looking).

Dory sat in row one. If her pop left, row one would be tied with row four.

She scowled at Fish. Looked back at the game. Pike already had two pawns home, and she had none. Which didn't feel so important all of a sudden.

Fish sat down across from Pop. "When I get to enlist, I'm hoping for the navy."

Pop shook his head. Even his own son, ready to answer the call. His blood had been running cold for months at the idea of Fish over there with the "floods of aggression." "Lord, I hope it doesn't come to that." He murmured it like a sort of a prayer.

Fish shrugged. "Only ten months, Pop, and I'll be old enough." He even knew a couple of boys from Seward Park High who'd lied about their ages and enlisted already. Fish wasn't quite prepared to go that far, but this time next year...

"I know, son. I know." Pop's voice was hoarse. "You're grown."

Dory wrinkled her nose. "He's not that grown."

"He's seventeen and one-sixth," Pike said. "And I'm seven and eleven-twelfths." Pike had a very good grasp of fractions for someone so young, but his missing front teeth made it difficult to say words like *twelfths*.

"Heck, Dory," Fish said, "Pop was only a year older than I am when he married Mama and had me."

Pop gave a dark chuckle. "It was a different time."

"I don't know, Pop. It's hard to think of a time that's more *different* than this one."

Pop sighed. "Fair enough." The war had turned everything on its head. "But, son..." He folded over the draft notice and creased it with his thumbnail, thinking about the dreams he'd nurtured for his children. The one about raising them in a world that had finally found some peace

11

after the Great War and the Great Depression (neither of which was great in the least)—that one certainly wasn't working out so far. But the one about them growing up to be something bigger and better than he was—maybe that dream still had a shot.

Was the notice on the kitchen table the answer?

Was it a sort of trade, Pop going?

If Fish were the man of the house, would he be saved from conscription?

If you looked at it that way, could Pop fight for both his country and his family at the same time?

He cleared his throat. "You're going places, Fisher." He didn't mean places like Germany and Japan, either, places where there was "wholesale murder" afoot. "You're gonna build ships one day. Not fight wars on them." He ran a hand through his hair. "And if I go now—"

Dory's head shot up like she'd been hit with an upper-cut. "But, Pop..." Her chest felt as if it were filled with hot coals. "You can't." She stood and crossed to the table, climbing onto his lap and burying her face in his scratchy neck.

A great big trench had grown between Fish's eyebrows. "Pop, I don't know if I..." He paused. "If we..." He trailed off, like the *I* and the *we* were jostling up against each other in his head. He looked down at the notice. "I always figured it would be me over there."

"But what if it wasn't?" Pop held Fish's gaze. "Could you manage without me?"

"I—" Fish started, and stopped again.

Dory wanted to finish for him. To say that he definitely could not manage. That none of them could. Fish was all right as big brothers went, she supposed, but she certainly didn't want him standing in for Pop. All she wanted Fish to do was take his turn at Sorry!, and then they could just forget about the paper on the kitchen table. Forget about the whole war, in fact.

As if wars could just be forgotten like that.

Pop stroked her hair. When he spoke, his voice was thin. "You wouldn't be on your own," he said. "The neighborhood..."

Pike rose and came to the table, crawling onto Fish's lap and finishing Pop's sentence for him. "The neighborhood will give us what we need."

The words were familiar because they'd all heard them a thousand times. Pop had lived on the Lower East Side his whole life. In a city of 7.5 million, it was a neighborhood of a mere 234,934 souls, making it much homier. And the Byrnes had been raised to believe in its essential goodness.

"That's right, Pike." Pop's smile was shaded with sorrow. (Many smiles were, in those days.)

Dory wasn't smiling at all. "It's not the same," she said.

"Of course it isn't." Pop nodded. "I'm not saying it is. But...Mrs. Schmidt would help out."

Dory scowled. "She's always telling me I oughta wear dresses."

Pop kissed the top of her head. "And Mrs. Kopek."

"She makes weird food," Dory said.

"And you know Mr. Bergen will always be there for you," Pop added.

Dory couldn't come up with any complaints about the landlord. He was famously kind. But she wasn't prepared to be gracious about anything just now. "Mr. Bergen could drop dead of a heart attack any minute. And then where would we be?"

"Dory!"

"I'm not wishing it." She buried her face in his neck again. "I'm just saying it's a possibility." She tightened her grip on the barrel of Pop's chest.

He stroked her hair with one hand, picked up the draft notice with the other. He looked at each of his children, his eyes landing last on Fish. "So could you?" he asked again. "Manage, I mean."

Feeling her father's heartbeat in the tender space between his jaw and collarbone, Dory waited for Fish to say no. To say that they should tear that draft notice into a thousand pieces and flush it down the toilet in the hallway bathroom outside the apartment, and then pinch one another to wake themselves up from this bad dream they all seemed to be having.

But what Fish said was, "Yeah, Pop. I mean...I...Yeah."

With her eyes squeezed shut against Pop's shoulder, Dory couldn't see how all the blood had drained from her brother's cheeks. How he bit his lower lip to stop it from trembling. All Dory knew was that Fish had just okayed the worst idea in the history of worst ideas.

(It was Pop's idea in the first place, of course. But

Pop was talking about heading off to the bloodshed. And you're not allowed to be angry at a person who's considering such a thing.)

None of them spoke for a long time. They all just sat there, thinking. All thinking about the same thing, though each of them did it in their own way.

Pop thought about the fact that *patriot* and *patriarch* sound sort of the same.

Fish thought about duty, and how his understanding of it had just been turned on its head.

Pike thought about whether Pop would be there to sing to him when he turned eight.

And Dory thought about how Susan Schneider in row three still looked pale and drawn, even a year after getting the news about her father.

Nothing was decided there and then, exactly.

But on November 15, the date on Pop's draft notice, he went to the appointed place at the appointed time.

He went to fight Hitler.

And a great big chunk of Dory Byrne's heart went with him.

✳

Which is why, now, five months later, Dory felt entirely justified in shouting at Fish about how this was all his fault and she'd been right about everything.

(She'd even been right about the landlord, though it was a fall from a ladder while taking down Christmas decorations, not a heart attack, that killed Mr. Bergen.)

Standing there, anger burning a hole in her rib cage, Dory looked at her brothers.

Fish pulled a graying handkerchief out of his pocket and held it to Pike's nose.

"Blow," he said.

Pike blew. Gave an all-done-crying sort of shudder.

And Dory felt the fire go out of her.

She swallowed. Steeled herself. Went to Pop's bedroom— Fish's bedroom since November—and retrieved Pop's favorite shirt. The flannel one with good, sturdy pockets on both sides. She put it on, wrapping herself tight in the closest thing she could get to a hug from her father.

She returned to the living room and lowered herself onto the worn sofa, blowsy with flowers and shot through with holes.

Fish carried Pike to the sofa and joined her, throwing an arm around each of them.

He sighed. "We're not doing so bad, are we?"

"What's for supper?" Pike asked.

"Corned beef."

Pike nuzzled into Fish's ribs. "Then we're not doing so bad."

"I brought crullers," Dory said, pointing to the bag on the sofa's arm.

Fish smiled down at her. "How many'd Mrs. Schmidt give you today?"

"Four, I think. She told me I should wear dresses. Again."

Fish squeezed her tight. "Nah. Don't change for anybody, Dor."

Dory nodded into his armpit.

"Except Pike," Fish added. "Change for Pike. Be responsible for him, okay?"

Dory nodded again. Her brother smelled like rain and kindness. "Is *Archie* on the radio tonight?"

"No," Pike said. "But there's *The Green Hornet*."

Dory sighed. "Then we're not doing so bad."

SOME SORT OF BENEFIT
OUT OF THE
ARRANGEMENT

Fish woke Dory and Pike the next morning, kissing Pike on his sleep-damp forehead, rubbing Dory's back until she stirred. High school started earlier than grammar school, and he had to walk all the way to Grand Street.

He squeezed Dory's shoulder. "You've got Pike again today, remember?"

Dory rolled over, her mouth thick with sleep. "Two days in a row?"

He nodded. "I've gotta drop off some papers at the Navy Yard after school." Fish had his fingers crossed for a shipbuilding apprenticeship at the Brooklyn Navy Yard. If he got it, he would start that summer and continue going after school in the fall, and by the time he graduated, he'd have a real job. Which was what Pop meant when he said Fish was going places. Even if, for now, the only place Fish wanted to go was Brooklyn.

"All right." Dory yawned. "I'll remember."

Fish shouldered his schoolbag and threw them a sloppy salute.

Dory and Pike heard the apartment door open and, for a few seconds, caught the din of the Tsitak twins in apartment 4. It was a whole floor down, but those babies had strong lungs. With Mr. Tsitak and Pop both away, the Byrnes and Mrs. Tsitak always exchanged sympathetic smiles when they passed at the mailboxes in the lobby. Mrs. Tsitak didn't speak any English, so a sympathetic smile was the best any of them could do.

Not that a sympathetic smile is an insignificant thing.

Dory rolled over again and wrapped her pillow around her head.

Pike got up from the double bed he had all to himself now that Fish had taken Pop's room. "Don't go back to sleep, Dory," he said.

"Okay." Her pillow-muffled voice was small.

Pike stood over her. "Like, not even a little bit."

"I won't. Just give me a sec."

Pike gave her exactly that. "Dory."

Rolling over with a groan, Dory dislodged a strand of hair from her mouth and sat up. "Okay, okay, okay!"

∗

Pike's insistence, while irritating, was justified.

In the first couple of weeks after Pop left for the war, Dory had rather taken advantage. Some days she got up. Some days she didn't. On those she didn't, she let Pike sleep in, too, then made them both bowls of farina, which they ate draped over the arms of the sofa, music burbling from the portable radio on the kitchen counter.

She told Pike to keep his mouth shut. What Fish didn't know wouldn't hurt him.

But when a letter arrived from PS 42 informing Mr. Byrne that Pike and Dory had missed four of the last ten school days, Fish's head about exploded. The conversation went something like this:

"Where's your brain, Dory?" he shouted.

Dory thought she could see actual steam coming out of his ears.

"What are you thinking, playing hooky like that?"

The truth was, Dory had been thinking that if she was going to have to do without Pop, she might as well get some sort of benefit out of the arrangement. But she didn't say that. She only put her hands on her hips and gave a huff.

"And bringing Pike into it?" Fish added.

"Pike didn't complain!"

"Of course he didn't complain!" Fish shouted. "That's beside the point."

Pike shrugged. "Dory makes good farina."

"I don't care if Dory baked you a triple-layer chocolate cake!" Fish sputtered. "You know school can't find out about Pop! Official types can't get wind of anything suspicious, and playing hooky is definitely suspicious! Do you want some truant officer or orphanage lady to come poking around here and ship you two off to the foundling home?"

Which...well.

Dory considered this for only a moment.

She and Pike never played hooky again.

✳

Satisfied that his sister was sufficiently roused, Pike bolted for the door. "I'm first in the bathroom," he said, already halfway there.

With the landlord's apartment vacant since January, it was only themselves using the hallway bathroom. Though none of them had ever thought twice about sharing with Mr. Bergen before he fell off the ladder and died. Down on the second floor, Mrs. Kopek was forever complaining about the Doyle sisters across the hall, how they left their unmentionables draped on the doorknob and hanging from the hinges in the bathroom. Dory wasn't sure what an unmentionable was, but she guessed Mr. Bergen must not have had any.

She gave a bellowing yawn and dislodged herself from her bedsheets. Ran her tongue over her teeth and grimaced. Padded into the kitchen and saw that Fish had left the last of Mrs. Schmidt's crullers for them on a chipped plate on the counter.

It was tempting to shove it, whole, into her mouth while Pike was otherwise occupied, but after yesterday's incident, guilt got the better of her. She set the pastry in the oven, contenting herself with licking grainy bits of crusted sugar off her fingers. She packed two peanut butter sandwiches in lunch sacks, then grabbed an apple from the near-empty bin in the cupboard, telling herself that an apple is every bit as good as a cruller.

(An apple is not as good as a cruller. Not by a long shot.)

Dory looked at the framed photograph of Pop and Mama—taken at Coney Island years ago—on the rickety table by the door. Her parents grinned black-and-white grins at her as she took a bite of her apple.

When Pike returned, she retrieved the warm cruller and handed it to him, glancing over his shoulder at Pop and Mama again.

She liked to think she was doing them proud.

✳

Their bellies somewhat fuller and their teeth somewhat cleaner, Pike and Dory headed for PS 42.

Despite her brief foray into truancy, Dory thought school was all right. There wasn't much of anything to dislike about it, she supposed. Generally speaking, there are only three reasons for a person to dislike school:

1. That person is not good at schoolish things.
2. That person is bullied by larger and/or meaner children.
3. That person is stuck with a shrewish teacher.

In Dory's case, none of the above reasons applied.

She was fairly capable when it came to schoolish things. Except arithmetic. With arithmetic, *fairly capable* was a stretch.

She wasn't bullied any more than your average twelve-year-old. Nor did she bully others, although there had been that one time in third grade when she'd dipped the ends of Ermaline Novak's braids in paste. But Ermaline—who sat in front of Dory that year—had such very dangly braids that the temptation was just too much.

And Dory's teacher, Miss Ozinskas, wasn't shrewish. She had the sort of soft voice and easy laugh that made sixth grade manageable. Which is really saying something, sixth grade being what it is.

So school was all right.

Dory delivered Pike to Mrs. Denton's second-grade classroom, room 119. Mrs. Denton wasn't a shrew, either. Though she did insist that children be allowed only two visits to the lavatory on any given day. Dory had had Mrs. Denton in second grade, so she knew about the bathroom limits from personal experience. Under normal circumstances, two trips a day was fine, but Dory had instructed Pike that if he ever had a real emergency, he should make a run for it and explain later rather than risking the embarrassment of an accident. Again, personal experience.

Checking the clock above the chalkboard in Pike's classroom, Dory saw that she had less than a minute to make it to the other side of PS 42 and up the three flights of stairs to room 403. She sighed, facing the age-old dilemma of whether to come in after the bell rang or risk being caught running in the halls by Miss O'Donnell, the (decidedly shrewish) assistant principal. Consequence-wise, it didn't much matter. Both crimes were punishable by an afternoon spent clapping erasers against PS 42's rear wall, out by the blacktop. It was a horrible job that left a person coughing the whole way home.

Dory pondered her limited options for a second or two and took off for the stairs at a run.

She made it to the stairwell, where she checked the clock across the hall, above the gymnasium door. Thirty-five seconds to go. She took the stairs three at a time, wishing—as always—that school allowed trousers. At the top, she grabbed the doorframe and used it to propel herself, whip-like, into the sixth-grade hallway.

Where she collided with Miss O'Donnell.

"Miss Byrne!" the assistant principal exclaimed.

Dory rubbed her shoulder. Miss O'Donnell sure had sharp elbows. "Sorry, Miss O'Donnell."

The morning bell rang.

The assistant principal stared down her nose through a pair of wire-rimmed glasses. "No running in the halls, Miss Byrne."

"Yes, ma'am." Dory scowled at her shoes.

"If you would be so kind as to join me in the front office, I will write you a tardy pass."

"Yes, ma'am."

"And then, this afternoon, I'll look forward to your help—"

"With the erasers." Dory sighed. "I know."

✳

Miss Ozinskas accepted Dory's tardy pass with a sympathetic smile and told her the class was about to get started with penmanship drills.

Dory slid into her seat in front of Vincent Morello.

"Erasers?" he whispered.

"Mm-hmm," Dory murmured.

Vincent cleared his throat. "I'll help you, if you want."

Dory was glad Vincent sat behind her in row one so she could have a conversation with him without making eye contact. Lately it seemed he was forever offering to do things for her—carry her books, trade items from their lunch sacks, give her a foil gum wrapper he'd found in the gutter for the scrap drive—and while all of it was very nice, and Vincent wasn't bad looking as sixth-grade boys went, the attention only made Dory's neck itch.

"I could walk you home, after," he added. Vincent's apartment was on Madison, the next block down from the Byrnes'.

"Thanks, Vincent." Dory levered open her desk's top and retrieved a sheet of paper. "But I'll be okay."

"Suit yourself," Vincent said. His voice cracked.

Dory scratched the back of her neck.

Penmanship should probably be added to the list of

schoolish things at which Dory did not excel. For the first half hour of the school day, she sat at her desk making an endless coil of cursive *e*'s and *l*'s. The loops were supposed to intersect in an orderly fashion, but Dory's tended to wobble. She found it helpful to hum the tune to "Praise the Lord and Pass the Ammunition" as she went, each loop reaching its apex with a beat of the tambourine in her head, but Joseph Ricci, in row two, kept giving her dirty looks. She didn't know whether it was her voice that bothered him, or whether he just didn't care for the song, but she stopped anyhow. Her *e*'s went saggier with every loop.

✳

Dory's seat was diagonal from Rosemary Manzetti's in row two. Dory and Rosemary had been friends since the second grade, when Dory told Rosemary she really liked her ringlet curls and Rosemary—quick as a wink—reached for a pair of scissors, cut off one of the perfect spirals, and handed it to Dory as a gift. The curl she'd cut had been right in the front, too, so there was no hiding it. Dory was pretty sure Mrs. Manzetti still blamed her for the incident.

In the past few months, though, Dory had started feeling a little distant from Rosemary. She found her mind wandering while Rosemary was talking about whatever Rosemary was talking about: the disastrous upside-down cake she'd made with her mother the night before, or something her father had seen at his volunteer job with the Air Raid Observation Service. Rosemary's dad had been declared unfit for military service because he had a bum leg. Before the war, Dory had always felt bad for Rosemary, having a dad who couldn't walk quite right, but now she'd give anything for her own pop to have a little thing like a limp.

So she guessed jealousy was at least part of the reason her friendship with Rosemary had cooled. Pure and simple jealousy. Which is not something that's terribly comfortable to admit about yourself.

"Want to come for dinner at my apartment tonight?" Rosemary asked as they ate their lunches together at their desks. "Ma's making spaghetti."

Dory took a bite of her sandwich. "Jeez, Rosemary. I'd love to, but it's Thursday."

The Byrnes were treated to seafood stew at Caputo's restaurant down by the fish market every Thursday. Mr. Caputo and Pop went way back, so Thursdays were Mr. Caputo's way of helping out after Pop left.

"Oh. Right. I forgot," Rosemary said. Official types might not be in on the Byrnes' living arrangement, but friends—and everybody else in the neighborhood—knew the score. "Another night?"

"Sure."

"How's Fisher?"

Rosemary always called Fish by his full name. Dory suspected she had a crush on him but had never asked. Imagine anybody being sweet on Fish. It was disgusting.

"He's all right."

"Next time Ma invites you for spaghetti, maybe you can all come?"

"Maybe." Dory changed the subject. "Did you listen to *The Green Hornet* last night?"

"Yeah. I didn't see that ending coming. Did you figure out the assistant wasn't really blind?"

"Nope. But Fish did."

Rosemary laughed. "Of course he did. He's practically a grown-up."

Dory's nose wrinkled on one side. "He's not that much of a grown-up."

"Sure he is. He's got muscles and everything."

Dory put down the last of her peanut butter sandwich.

"Are you gonna go to the sixth-grade dance?" Rosemary asked.

"That's not for three weeks."

Rosemary licked salt from a hard-boiled egg. "It's never too soon to think about it."

Dory wasn't sure that was true at all. "Anyhow, probably not."

"How come?"

Dory shrugged. "I don't know how to dance."

"So? Neither do I. Neither does most of the sixth grade." Rosemary glanced over her shoulder, where Vincent Morello was throwing his waxed paper into the wastepaper basket. "Besides—I know for a fact that Vincent wants to ask you to dance."

Dory's breath caught in her throat. "How do you know that?"

Rosemary raised her eyebrows. "He told me."

"He told you? Jeez Louise!"

Rosemary looked over her shoulder again. Vincent was still by the wastepaper basket, looking at a comic with Ernest Klein now. "Yes, and I think you should go."

"Are you going?"

"Of course."

"And are you going to dance with anybody?" Dory asked.

Rosemary wiped her mouth with the knuckle of her index finger. "Probably Ronald DeMarco."

"Ronald?" Dory glanced sideways toward the back corner, where Ronald was surreptitiously picking his nose. Which made Dory think that, if he were her dance partner, she wouldn't be terribly excited about holding his hand.

"Yeah." Rosemary's cheeks flushed pink. "Well, will you come? Please?"

Dory folded her hands on her desk and rested her chin on them. "What would I wear?" She knew she wouldn't be allowed in wearing trousers, and her closet wasn't exactly bursting with party dresses.

"Borrow something of mine," Rosemary said.

Dory sighed.

Rosemary bounced up and down in her seat. "So it's decided."

"Wait," Dory said. "Nothing's decided."

Rosemary grinned. "I'll convince you somehow."

Vincent returned to his seat, giving Dory an eager smile as he passed.

Her neck itched something awful.

*

Dory collected Pike from room 119 after school and told him about the erasers.

"Aw, nuts, Dory," he said. "Can't you go a week without getting in trouble?"

"I've gone plenty longer than a week!" Dory crossed her arms over her chest, counting back the days in her head. She was pretty sure it had been almost two weeks, in fact.

Pike gave a slow shake of his head. "I just helped you clap erasers last Friday."

Had it really been only Friday? Dory squeezed her eyes shut and thought hard. Right. Friday was the day Miss Ozinskas had asked her to deliver a note to Miss O'Donnell. When you visited the assistant principal's office, you had to write your name on a paper whose instructions read SIGN IN TO LET MISS O'DONNELL KNOW THE REASON FOR YOUR VISIT. It was impossible for Dory to resist the temptation to pencil an *i* between the *to* and the *let*.

So Pike was right as usual. "Fine. It was Friday. But the only reason I was late this morning was because I warmed up that cruller for you."

Pike gave a half smile. "Fair enough." The smile faded. "But I don't feel like clapping again today."

"No buts, Pike. We don't have a choice."

30

"I have a choice. It's *you* that doesn't have a choice."

Dory grabbed his hand and dragged him down the hall. "Well, you need me to get home, so I guess that means you don't have a choice, either."

"I can go to the library and wait for you. I even walked home yesterday all by myself."

Dory led him out the front door and down the steps. "Yeah, and you left snot all over Fish's shoulder."

Pike scowled. "Billy Donnelly walks home by himself."

"Billy Donnelly's a drip."

"He's not a drip."

They walked to the blacktop on the back side of PS 42. "Wasn't it just last month that he stole a frog from Mrs. Denton's terrarium and set it loose in the teachers' lounge?"

"It was a toad."

Dory turned to face her brother. "Listen, Pike. I don't want to get in hot water with Fish for abandoning you again. You don't have to help me, but you have to wait with me until I'm done." She could see Miss O'Donnell rounding the corner, carrying a wide metal tub of erasers. It looked like enough erasers to clean every chalkboard on the Lower East Side.

Pike turned to see what she was staring at. "That's an awful lot of erasers."

"Uh-huh."

"Fine." Pike exhaled dramatically. "I'll help you."

DUMBWAITER

Caputo's Fine Seafood had been a fixture in the Fulton Fish Market neighborhood since Pop was young. The building that housed it had been constructed nearly a hundred years ago. Aged bricks rose five stories to a gabled roof whose windows must have offered a perfect view of the Brooklyn Bridge a few blocks north, only they'd been boarded up since who-knows-when. Sandwiched between Sable's Fisherman's Supplies and Sam's Bargain Shop, Caputo's did a steady lunch and dinner business with the longshoremen, vendors, and fishermen who kept the machine of the wholesale market district running. Monday through Friday, Mr. Caputo rolled out the green-striped awning around ten in the morning and cranked it back in around eight in the evening, when the market was shuttered, the surrounding blocks vacant, and Mr. Caputo said it was time to go home and smoke a pipe with his wife. (It was only him smoking. Mrs. Caputo didn't care for the stuff.)

When Dory, Pike, and Fish went to Caputo's on Thursday nights, it was generally about an hour before closing. The bell above the restaurant door jangled like it was Christmastime, which made the place feel friendly. Its ceilings were low and its lighting poor, lending it some coziness, Dory thought. And the scent of seafood stew hung so thick in the air that it felt like being in the ocean.

Mr. Caputo seemed permanently angry. His unreasonable eyebrows hung low over his eyes, giving the impression of a scowl. And his voice was a continual shout. A bark, almost. He barked at the waitresses. He barked at the busboys. He barked at the customers.

"Francie! Wipe that up before somebody slips!"

"Angelo! You break one more bowl and I'll wring your neck!"

"Sit! Sit! Sit! You're letting the chill in!"

That last was what he barked at the Byrnes as they stood in the narrow doorway, Fish ushering Pike and Dory through, closing the door behind them, and nudging them to their usual table in the front window before yelling back thanks to Mr. Caputo.

Mr. Caputo wasn't really angry. Some people give off that impression as a sort of protection. A shell. Like a turtle's shell protects its soft underbelly. In his heart, Mr. Caputo was all soft underbelly. All kindness. But you don't run a busy restaurant for twenty-something years without doing a little shouting.

"Can I have a pickle?" Pike asked.

"Not tonight," Fish said.

Pike put his chin on the sticky table. "Not any night."

Fish looked out the window onto South Street, where a skin-and-bones cat gnawed on a fish head. "It's free food, Pike. Don't complain." Fish always told Dory and Pike they weren't allowed to order anything extra because Mr. Caputo was already being generous with the seafood stew. Fish believed what Pop always said about the neighborhood giving them what they needed, but there were lines he wouldn't cross. And one of the lines was pickles.

"I talked to Mrs. Kopek this afternoon," Fish said, "when I was picking up the paper."

Mrs. Kopek shared her newspaper with the Byrnes so they could keep up with war news.

"Did she complain about the bunnies on her feet?" Pike asked.

"Of course she did." Fish grinned. "Mrs. Kopek's bunions are eternal." Then his face went serious. "She thinks we oughta take Pop's flag out of the window."

"What?" Dory gasped. "Why?"

The service flag was a point of pride. A badge of honor telling the whole world—or at least anybody who could see your window—that someone in your family was doing their duty. The windows of the Lower East Side were full of them, blue stars showing that somebody was off fighting, and gold ones showing that somebody had died doing so.

Nobody wanted a gold one.

"Because the new landlord's supposed to arrive soon." Fish leaned forward. "Mrs. Kopek said we should check him out before we let on about Pop being gone."

"It wouldn't feel right," Dory said, "taking it down."

"I know," Fish said. "But I can see what Mrs. Kopek means. What if the new landlord isn't like Mr. Bergen?"

Pike nodded. "You mean, what if he's a meanie?"

"Exactly," Fish said. "What if he's a meanie?" He gave Dory an understanding smile. "We'll take it down tonight and hang it inside the apartment for now. You can decide where."

Dory didn't have time to think about where, because Mr. Caputo appeared with their dinners. Three bowls of stew, three spoons, three napkins, and three glasses of milk on a tray.

He unloaded the bowls first. "Everything good, bambini?"

Bambini was what Mr. Caputo called the Byrnes. It meant "children" in Italian, but every time Dory heard Mr. Caputo say it, she thought of the movie about the deer. Pop had taken the three of them to see it at the Century when it came out a couple of years ago. During the scene where Bambi wanders through the snow, calling for his mother, Pike started crying and Pop had to take him out to the lobby, leaving Dory and Fish alone for the part where Bambi's father tells him that his mother won't be coming back. Dory and Fish walked out at that point and never did see the second half. Dory didn't think her feelings had anything to do with her mama.

She just thought the movie was too horrible for anybody to watch, mama or not. Give her a good monster picture any day—vampires, werewolves, that kind of thing—but *Bambi*? Nope.

"We're swell, Mr. Caputo," Fish said.

Mr. Caputo set the last glass of milk on the table and threw up a hand. "Swell! I don't understand a word you kids say." He lowered the calloused hand to Pike's head, still nestled on the table atop his folded arms. "What's the matter, little Byrne?"

Pike raised his head and looked accusingly at Fish. "I want a pickle."

"Pike!" Fish said.

"A pickle?" Mr. Caputo shouted. He tucked the empty tray under his arm and gave Pike a sideways grin. "A pickle for Pike, eh?"

Fish nudged Pike's knee under the table. "Sorry, Mr. Caputo."

"No need for *sorry*," Mr. Caputo said, shaking his head. "A pickle we can do." It was hard to tell with all the eyebrows, but Dory was pretty sure she saw him wink as he turned and headed for the kitchen.

Pike looked at his brother and grinned.

A busboy passed with a tray of dirty dishes. Dory saw half a slice of what looked like cherry strudel on one and had to sit on her hands to keep from reaching out and snatching it. Desserts, like pickles, were against Fish's rules.

Dory slurped stew from her spoon and swiped at her mouth with her sleeve.

"Napkin!" Fish said. "Jeez Louise, Dory."

There was more shouting from the kitchens. "Stack those trays, Angelo! Not there! By the dumbwaiter!"

Pike giggled. "Dumb waiter."

Dory and Fish smiled.

"A dumbwaiter's like an elevator for dishes, isn't it?" Dory asked.

Fish nodded.

She sipped her milk. "What would you need a dish elevator for, if the kitchen and the restaurant are on the same floor?"

Fish shrugged. "Ask Mr. Caputo."

Right on cue, Mr. Caputo approached from the kitchen with another tray. He raised his caterpillar eyebrows at the Byrnes, cocked a sideways smile at Pike, and unloaded a perfect dill pickle on a saucer, along with three plates of cherry strudel.

Dory beamed. Which is something Dory Byrne very rarely did.

"Aw, thanks, Mr. Caputo," Fish said. "You didn't have to do that."

Mr. Caputo grunted. "There were some leftovers." It doesn't sound like an especially heartfelt thing to say, but that was how the children took it.

"Thanks, Mr. Caputo." Pike's mouth was already full of pickle.

Dory pushed her seafood stew aside for now and took a bite of strudel. The tender layers of pastry and fruit melted on her tongue. "Do you ever use the dumbwaiter, Mr. Caputo?"

"Swallow first, Dor," Fish said.

Mr. Caputo shook his head. "That old thing? Never."

"What's it there for, anyhow?" Dory asked. "With the kitchen and the restaurant both right here on the ground floor?"

"Well," Mr. Caputo said, "the truth of the matter is, it isn't a usual sort of a dumbwaiter. It's a hand-elevator, sure. The rope-pull kind. But it's meant for people, not dishes."

"For people?"

"Well, it was." Mr. Caputo nodded. "Back when this place was first built, in the olden days. But nobody's been in that thing since I opened the restaurant."

"How long's that?" Dory asked.

He looked at the ceiling, counting the years. "I signed the lease in 1923, so that's what now—twenty-one years?"

"Twenty-one years?"

"Well, that's just when I got here. Before that, who knows?"

Dory squinted at him. "How come?"

"How come what?" Mr. Caputo asked.

"How come nobody's been in it?"

"You got a lotta questions, bambina." Mr. Caputo ran a hand through his thinning gray hair. "Nobody's been in it because nobody wants to *get* in it. That thing's been around since the last century. Ropes have probably gone to rot."

"So everybody just takes the stairs now?"

Mr. Caputo nodded again. "To the second floor, sure. I use the second floor for storage. The stairs only go that far."

Dory narrowed her gaze. "What do you mean?"

"Jesus, Mary, and Joseph, with the questions. The stairs only go to the second floor. After that, the dumb-waiter's the only way up."

Now Pike was interested. "Why would somebody make a building that way?"

Mr. Caputo pulled up a chair and sat. "I think it happened sort of by accident. This building and the one next door—what's now Sable's—they were built together, essentially as one building, connected by a kind of a party wall, is what I've been told."

"What's a party wall?" Pike asked.

"Used to be, there were doors between this building and that one, on every floor. But they were all bricked up years ago. And the stairs were over on that side, leaving this side with only the dumbwaiter to access the third, fourth, and fifth floors."

Dory pondered this for a moment. "What's on those other floors?"

"No idea."

Her eyes goggled.

"No idea?" Fish asked.

Mr. Caputo grinned. "Nope."

Dory nearly dropped her fork. "Aren't you curious?"

"Sure." Mr. Caputo gave a playful grimace. "But I'm also a chicken."

"What if there's something good up there, though?" Pike asked.

"Yeah. Like money," Dory said.

"Or candy," Pike added.

Fish shook his head. "You really want to eat candy that's been sitting around twenty or thirty years, Pike?"

Pike shrugged. "I bet Life Savers still taste good that long. And probably Red Hots."

Dory thought Pike's line of questioning was irrelevant. She didn't even like Red Hots. "Where is it, Mr. Caputo?"

"The dumbwaiter?" The old man gestured toward the back hallway. "Back there, across from the stairs. Between the restroom and the kitchen."

Dory had used Caputo's restroom a hundred times. She'd never noticed the dumbwaiter. "Can I see?"

Mr. Caputo grunted. Grunting was something he did quite often. "See? What do you mean, *see*? There's nothing to see. Just a cracked wooden door that leads to a dark shaft. It's filthy," he said. "And dangerous," he added, giving Dory a long, hard look. "Don't even think about it, bambina."

But it was too late.

Dory was already thinking about it.

*

She talked about it with Libby after school the next day. Libby never talked back, of course—she was only a statue, after all—but sometimes Dory imagined what she might say if she did. Besides, Dory found it helpful just to speak her own thoughts out loud. And she had an awful lot of thoughts about the ancient dumbwaiter and the three whole floors that nobody'd seen in years and years and years.

She raised Pop's binoculars and squinted out at the Green Goddess. She'd been to Libby's home on Bedloe's Island a few times on class trips and had written a report about her last year, so she knew a lot about the statue. Knew, for example, that before she came to New York Harbor, Libby's head—just her head—was put on display in Paris. It was deliciously creepy.

"What the heck could be up there on the floors above Caputo's?" She lowered the binoculars. "I mean, the place is about a million years old. Do you think there could be pirate treasure?"

Dory figured Libby knew a lot about pirates, her being on the water and all. Seven spikes on her crown. Seven oceans.

"Maybe dead bodies?" Dory shivered.

Dead bodies made her think of Pop, off fighting. And of Mama. Which got her thinking of something else she knew about the statue: people said her face was meant to look like the sculptor's mother. That made Dory's heart feel warm.

Her thoughts returned to the dumbwaiter. And whatever it led to.

She had to figure out a way to get into it.

She just had to.

THE MARVELING

On Saturday, Dory convinced her brothers to make the almost three-mile trek north to the Empire State Building. The trekking part didn't take much convincing. Just seeing the glittering monstrosity up close was worth a blister or two. But Dory wanted to go to the top, and getting to the top was another story. Tickets to the observatory cost a dollar apiece, and that was a whole lot of clams, as Fish put it. A dollar was enough clams, in fact, to buy any of the following:

- Eight pounds of apples
- Thirty-three postage stamps
- Eleven loaves of bread
- Ten bars of Ivory soap
- Two tickets to a baseball game (but just for the minor league across the river in

New Jersey—if you wanted to see the
Yankees, a dollar would buy you only one
ticket)

"Three dollars is too much," Fish said as they crossed Houston.

"But we should be getting another letter from Pop soon," Dory said.

Pop's letters—and the money that came with them—arrived, like clockwork, the last week of every month. The children's letters back were just as regular and twice as frequent.

"Yeah, but still," Fish said. He crouched low to let Pike ride piggyback. "Three dollars is way too much." Fish was careful with the money that remained after the rent was paid. He kept it in an empty mayonnaise jar on top of the Frigidaire and doled it out only as needed.

"Fine," Dory said. She had a plan to get them to the top, but she couldn't help thinking about Caputo's secret floors. The way she figured it, there was probably enough treasure up there to buy a million trips to the top of the Empire State Building. Buy the whole skyscraper, even.

Her thoughts returned to Pop. "In his last letter it didn't sound like he'd been doing a lot of fighting."

Fish looked sideways at her. "Maybe he just didn't want us to worry."

"You think he was lying?"

"Well, not so much lying," Fish said. "More...protecting."

"Like Captain America," Pike said.

"Yeah. Like Captain America." Fish hiked Pike higher on his back.

They walked in silence for a good many blocks, crossing Union Square Park and continuing onto Broadway. Past the Flatiron Building, then another eleven blocks up Fifth.

"How much farther?" Pike asked.

Fish stopped and set him on his feet. "Look up."

And there it was. The tallest building in the whole wide world.

Pop had always called it a tourist trap. And maybe it was, but Dory couldn't help feeling just a little more important, looking up at its famous height. She'd had nothing to do with it, of course, but she liked to think that such audacity could only come from a city like New York.

Her city.

She shielded her eyes with her hand and looked up. "Wow." She gave a low whistle. "How tall do you figure it is, exactly?"

"One thousand, four hundred, and fifty-four feet," Pike said.

Dory squinted at him. "How do you know?"

Pike shrugged. "The library."

"So here's what I'm thinking," Dory said. "We're going to stand in the lobby and watch people coming off the elevators. We need to find the three sweetest-looking tourists in New York. Old ladies'll probably work best."

Fish looked skeptical. "And what are you going to do to them?"

"I'm not going to do anything to them. Just ask them for their tickets." She squinted at her brothers. "But, Pike, you're going to need to cry."

Pike put his hands on his hips. "What?"

"What?" Fish echoed.

"For sympathy," Dory explained. "So they'll give us their used-up tickets."

"No way," Fish said.

"I'll do the talking, Fish. All you need to do is look worried, just like right now."

"I look worried because I *am* worried," Fish said.

Dory grinned. "Keep up the good work."

"I can't just cry for no reason," Pike protested.

"It's not for no reason," Dory said. "It's to get us to the top of the Empire State Building."

"I mean, I can't just start crying without having anything to cry about."

"Want me to pinch you?"

Pike recoiled. "No!"

"Dory," Fish said, "even if we got some little old ladies to give us their tickets, we can't use them. Ticket-takers tear those things up so everybody knows they're no good anymore."

"Which is why Pike has to cry. People get discombobulated when a cute little kid starts crying. It throws them off their game."

"I won't do it," Pike said.

Dory weighed her options. Fish was no use in the crying

department. Even if he could turn on the waterworks—
which was doubtful—he was too old. It wouldn't have the
same effect.

"Fine," she said. "I'll do it."

"But, Dory—" Fish started.

She interrupted him. "Look, we just walked about a
gazillion blocks. Did you come all that way to stand in
the lobby?"

Fish squinted at her. "Listen, Dor. Maybe we could
splurge on subway fare home, instead. The subway'd be
fun, wouldn't it?"

Pike looked up at the great beast of a skyscraper. "I
want to go to the top." He scowled at his sister. "But Dory's
gotta do the crying."

So she did.

It was all quite impressive, to tell you the truth.

Dory found her mark in a group of ladies who emerged
from the elevator wide-eyed and smiling. From their
overheard conversation, which included the phrase *land
sakes*, she could tell they weren't from New York.

She looked at Fish, who was carrying Pike, his head
buried in his older brother's neck just in case he started
giggling and ruined everything.

She nodded. Fish nodded back.

For a girl who didn't go in much for squishy things like
feelings, the crying part came surprisingly easy. Dory found
that all she needed to do was think about the injustices in
her life. Injustices like her being unable to afford a trip to

the top of a skyscraper in her very own city. Like Hitler and all the wickedness that went along with him. Like Pop going off to fight him. And there they were—tears.

She picked the kindest-looking lady—a grandmotherly sort in a bonnet-shaped hat with daisies on the brim—and approached, wiping her eyes with the heel of her hand.

She sniffled. "Excuse me, ma'am?"

The bonnet lady glanced at her companions, then at Dory, her brow creased. "Yes, dear?"

"We . . . My brothers and me"—she looked at Fish and Pike—"got separated from our folks and can't get on the elevators because our papa has our tickets." She gave a coughing sort of a sob that she thought sounded heartbreakingly realistic.

"Oh, heavens! Poor mites!" Bonnet looked sympathetically at Fish and Pike and gathered Dory to her chest in a squashy hug.

Dory winced. Yikes. She hadn't anticipated hugging.

Once released, she gathered herself and swiped at her nose. "Would you give us your tickets, please, just so we can get back to our folks?" The thought occurred to Dory that any folks worth their salt would be back in the lobby as soon as they could catch the next elevator, not enjoying the view from the eighty-sixth floor wondering when their kids might figure a way to get themselves to the top. So her story had some holes in it.

Which was where the crying came in handy. She bit her tongue and heaved another sloppy sob. "Please, will you help us?"

"Of course! Of course, dear!" Bonnet exclaimed, looking to her companions. "But you needn't worry about using our tickets! I'll just have a word with the ticket man and the three of you will be back to your mama and papa just as quick as a wink!"

That would be something, Dory thought—if Bonnet could really get them back to their mama and papa. "Thank you, ma'am," she whispered.

"Yes, thank you, ma'am," Fish echoed. His voice cracked.

Dory wasn't sure whether he was acting or not, but either way it was effective.

Bonnet bustled them to the front of the elevator line, where she approached the tired-looking ticket man and informed him that this was an emergency and that these children needed to be put on the very next elevator so they could be reunited with their family.

The ticket man didn't so much as blink. He undid the hook on a velvet rope and ushered the children into an elevator. Dory, Pike, and Fish turned to thank Bonnet again, only to find her ferreting around in her pocketbook and producing a crisp new dollar bill.

She handed it to Dory. "Buy yourselves some ice creams at the top and tell your folks it's my treat. They must be beside themselves with worry. Hurry along now!"

She waved at the Byrnes, who only blinked at her, astonished, as the doors slid closed.

They hardly even noticed the elevator ride. Crammed like sardines in a can, all they could do was gape at one another. Dory clutched the dollar Bonnet had given her and felt a pang at the unexpected and—let's face it—undeserved benevolence. Tears welled in the corners of her eyes without any thoughts of injustice at all.

Around the sixty-third floor, her ears clogged the way they did when she had a head cold. She held her nose and blew to clear the pressure. Fish forced a yawn—which Pike promptly caught—to do the same. The doors opened at the eighty-sixth-floor observatory.

And there they were.

On the tippy top of the world.

Pike was first out the doors onto the observation platform, where the wind made him lose his balance and stumble backward into Dory.

"Jeepers, Pike, you'll blow away!" Fish laid a firm hand on his brother's shoulder.

The three of them ran for the railing and peered over the side. A million miles down, Dory could see cockroach taxicabs and flea people. To the north, Central Park unfolded in endless green. The city beyond that was another planet. Inwood. Washington Heights. Harlem. Hunt's Point. All those neighborhoods she'd never seen. Dory wondered if people from Washington Heights, so impossibly far away, ever thought about the Lower East Side.

Pike pulled on Fish's shirt. "Lift me up so I can see!"

Dory looked at her brothers, their cheeks pink from the stinging wind. She could feel the pink in her own cheeks. She grinned at the two of them, and they grinned back, teeth and all.

When they'd had their fill of the view to the north, they made their way to the other side of the observatory platform.

"I wonder if we can see our apartment," Pike said.

Squashing his head against his brother's, Fish pointed downtown. "See the Manhattan Bridge, there, and the Brooklyn Bridge just past it?"

Pike nodded.

"Our apartment's smack in the middle, just a couple of blocks from the river."

Pike squinted for a long moment. "I can see it!"

Dory and Fish exchanged glances. No way could he see any such thing. But neither one of them was about to ruin it for him.

Dory inhaled deeply, the air wild and plentiful. On the ground, she was used to being assaulted by smells. Bakeries, hot dogs, chestnuts, the harbor. Also garbage, exhaust, dead fish, her own unwashed socks. On top of the world, there was nothing. Dory wondered if this was what heaven smelled like.

She looked southwest and found Libby. The Green Goddess looked small and lonely on her island. Dory gave a surreptitious wave.

From there, she gazed east. Toward Europe. Toward Pop.

Then back at the statue. *Tell him that from way up here I can almost see him.*

"Holy mackerel," Fish whispered. He threw his free arm around her shoulder.

And there they stood for the longest time. Just marveling.

Which is something a person doesn't get a chance to do that often. Marvel.

✳

The marveling had such a strange effect on Fish, he let them splurge on both the nickel-apiece subway fare downtown and two containers of matzo ball soup from Aaronson's Delicatessen to carry home for dinner.

Hoping this month's letter from Pop had arrived early, they entered the apartment building the way regular people do, so they could check their mailbox in the lobby. Calling it a lobby was a stretch, really. It was more of a cramped hallway, the entrance to the stairwell on one side and built-in mailboxes for the building's six apartments on the other.

Fish handed Dory the soup containers to get the mailbox key out of his pocket. Pike stood on tiptoe, and he and Dory both leaned in, hoping to be the first to see Pop's letter.

But the box was empty.

Fish smiled at Pike and Dory. "It'll come soon," he said. "Next week, for sure."

Dory nodded. "Yeah." But the disappointment of the empty mailbox hit her in her heart somehow. Turning quickly toward the stairwell entrance so her brothers couldn't see that the disappointment was threatening to spill out the corners of her eyes, she smacked right into an unfamiliar man heading out of it. Smacked into him so hard, in fact, that she dropped one of the containers, sending matzo ball soup everywhere.

Everywhere.

It splashed onto the lobby wall, setting a sliver of carrot sliding down the molding around the stairwell entrance. It puddled on the worn lobby carpet, parsley-flecked broth spreading every which way. And a plump and perfect matzo ball landed with a volcanic squelch.

Right on the unfamiliar man's left shoe.

Dory looked up at him, horrified. "Jeez, mister, I'm sorry."

The man removed a foul-smelling cigar from the corner of his mouth and muttered several words Dory had heard the longshoremen use when she passed them at the docks on her way back from visiting Libby. When he was done muttering, he looked at the three of them.

His nostrils flared. "You kids live here?"

"Yes, sir," Fish said.

The man shook his head. "Great. That's just great."

Dory didn't understand what was so great about it. She had no idea who this man was, but she sure didn't like the look of him. His skin had a grayish hue to it, and his eyes were so dark and cold, they made him look like Bela Lugosi in *The Return of the Vampire*.

"Byrne, I assume?" The man shook his left foot, launching the matzo ball into the wall with a splat.

A sinking feeling bubbled in Dory's guts. Bela Lugosi knew their name.

"Yes, sir," Fish said again.

"I'm Mr. Reedy." The man's scowl deepened. "I'm your new landlord."

Dory's blood ran cold.

A vampire is not something you want your landlord to remind you of.

*

So Mrs. Kopek was right about being careful.

Because, if first impressions hold any water, the new landlord did appear to be a meanie.

Dory was able to get the evidence of the soup incident off the wall with a dishrag, but even though she lugged a bucket of soapy water downstairs to scrub the lobby carpet three times, the stain remained. As did the smell.

After such an inauspicious beginning, Dory conceded that their decision to take Pop's service flag out of the window and hang it inside the apartment on Thursday night had been a good one. So there it stayed, on the wall inside the apartment door, just over the rickety table with the Coney Island photograph of Pop and Mama.

*

Pop's letter arrived on Tuesday. The sight of his angular scrawl there on the page always squeezed Dory's heart. Looking at ink that had come out of a pen that had been in Pop's hand almost made her feel like she was holding that hand. She didn't say so out loud because it sounded corny, but she always thought it.

The letter was dated nearly three weeks ago. It was a single page, the words filling every bit of space on the front and back. Fish read it out loud to them. Dory saw his eyes go swimmy when he read Pop's usual greeting: "My Beloveds."

Pop's letters were full of stories. He told them about the sailor who talked in his sleep. The one who fell out of his bunk during a storm. About taking watch between midnight and four in the morning, how he had to pinch himself to keep from falling asleep standing up. About how much he missed them. "You're all I think about out here, day and night, night and day," he wrote.

Just like in his other letters, Pop didn't talk about fighting or where "out here" was, exactly. The children knew he was somewhere near Europe, but if you look on a map, you'll find that Europe is really a very big place.

Fish said Pop had to be cagey in describing his whereabouts. Before being sent, soldiers' letters were read by their ranking officers and censored as needed because "loose lips might sink ships."

"What's that mean?" Pike asked.

"It means that if Pop blabbed about where he is, the Nazis might overhear," Fish explained.

Pike frowned. "It's not blabbing if it's only to us."

"Yeah, but what if his letter got intercepted by Hitler, chucklehead?" Dory asked.

"Don't call me a chucklehead."

"Yeah, don't, Dor," Fish added, poking Dory in the

ribs. "But she's right, Pike. Pop's gotta be careful what he says, in case the mail falls into the wrong hands."

Dory ran her finger over Pop's handwriting for the hundredth time, the letter a sort of talisman, warming her heart at a touch. In her head, she composed the one she'd write back via Victory Mail, the military's solution to the glut of letters between servicemen and their families, a flood so vast it threatened to swamp supply ships. Letters were written on special paper, then photographed, put onto reels, and reprinted for delivery at V-Mail facilities overseas. The ads said:

KEEP HIM
POSTED...
MAKE IT SHORT
MAKE IT CHEERFUL
SEND IT...
V-MAIL

Dory sighed. Sometimes the *cheerful* part sure was a challenge.

✳

She thought about the dumbwaiter all week. The dumbwaiter, and whatever it led to. Pirate treasure was out of the question, she figured. In pictures, pirates were usually found on islands with palm trees on them. Manhattan was an island, but not the palm-tree kind.

She asked Pike about it, though, one afternoon when they were walking home. Pike knew stuff. Probably because of the library, Dory guessed.

"There've been plenty of pirates here," he said. "Captain Kidd, even."

Dory was flabbergasted. "Captain Kidd lived in New York?"

"Yeah. Just a couple of blocks away from here. On Pearl or Wall Street or something." He thought for a second. "And there was a real bad one named Albert W. Hicks, too. He got hanged, right out on Bedloe's Island."

"Wait," Dory said, her eyes wide. "They hung a pirate on Lib—" She stopped herself. She'd never told her brothers how she talked to the statue. Called her Libby. "They hung a pirate out there by the Statue of Liberty?"

"Well, it was before the statue's time, but yeah," Pike said. "And it's *hanged*, not *hung*."

Which was exasperating. But Pike's fund of knowledge was proving enticing.

✳

At Caputo's that Thursday, Dory decided she had to see the dumbwaiter for herself. At least the entrance to it. After she and the boys had taken off their sweaters and hung them on the backs of their chairs, she announced that she had to go to the bathroom. Mr. Caputo had said that the dumbwaiter was back there.

She looked over her shoulder to see where he was,

spotting him near the front door, shouting at a man in dockworkers' boots to hurry up and not let the chill in.

Ducking into the narrow back hall, Dory tried to look innocent.

Looking innocent while trying to find something you've been told in no uncertain terms to forget about is awfully difficult to do. In fact, Dory looked the opposite of innocent. But nobody seemed to be paying any attention. Busboys and waitresses bustled past with their trays.

Their trays! Dory distinctly remembered Mr. Caputo shouting at one of the busboys to stack the trays by the dumbwaiter. Her eyes landed on a pile of serving trays on a folding stand. She looked over her shoulder again and approached.

There, behind the stand, was a door. A cracked wooden one with a pair of rusted hinges on one side and an even-more-rusted closure—the kind that looks like an airplane propeller—on the other. The door was about six feet tall and four feet wide. Just right for a person or two.

Dory gasped. This was it. This was certainly, definitely, positively it.

Her eyes wandered up the wall. All she could see was the crack-webbed ceiling of Caputo's back hall. But in her imagination, she pictured all the riches that could be stashed above her. Three whole floors nobody'd seen in years and years and years. She simply had to know what sort of treasure they contained. In that moment, Dory realized three things:

1. She'd have to try out the dumbwaiter when Caputo's was closed, which meant that
2. She'd have to figure how to sneak in and hide while Caputo's was still open, and then
3. She'd have to spend the night.

IF YOU'RE GOING
TO DANCE WITH
SOMEBODY

With the arrival of May the following week, the only thing PS 42's sixth grade could talk about was the dance. According to Fish, all anybody did at sixth-grade dances was stand around in uncomfortable clothes. Which was unappealing, to say the least. But it seemed Dory was the only one who thought so.

The week of the dance, Miss O'Donnell came in to ask the children of room 403 if they had a parent who might like to chaperone. Dory's heart gave a lurch as she saw the hands go up, knowing she didn't have any parents around at all, let alone one who'd like to chaperone the sixth-grade dance.

Rosemary was persistent in her efforts to kindle Dory's enthusiasm. And Rosemary, as it turned out, was the inspiration behind Dory's plan to sneak into Caputo's. Not that Dory said anything about the plan, of course.

She didn't breathe a word about it to a single soul. But when Rosemary asked for the third time in as many days whether she would come to the dance, a sort of light switch flipped in Dory's head.

"You know what? Sure."

Rosemary beamed. "Oh, swell! Come to my house after school on Friday and we can get ready together. I'll do your hair!"

Dory wrinkled her nose. "What are you gonna do to it?"

"Don't you think pin curls would look nice on you?"

"I suppose." The most Dory had ever done to her hair was tuck it behind her ears.

"And I think Ma will let us use her lipstick."

That dumbwaiter better lead to some extremely valuable treasure, Dory thought, if she was going to have to resort to wearing lipstick.

"Okay." She gulped.

Rosemary bounced in her seat. "I can't wait!"

"Me neither. I just have to tell Fish."

Lie to Fish was what she really meant.

Her feelings about being minded by her brother notwithstanding, Dory didn't like lying to Fish. To anybody, really. Except when it was necessary. Which, it turned out, had been true of an awful lot of things since Pop left. Lying about the dumbwaiter, for example, was necessary. It was clearly, definitely, and extraordinarily necessary.

So she lied. As follows: "Fish, Rosemary asked me to sleep over on Friday after the dance. Can I?"

"Sure."

It was that easy.

*

And that was how Dory found herself standing in the school gymnasium, wearing a scratchy plaid party dress borrowed from Rosemary, leaning against the concrete wall with a pack of other girls with sweaty armpits, looking across the lacquered floor at the line of similarly arrayed and similarly sweaty boys. Glenn Miller's "In the Mood" burbled in the background.

Dory resisted the twin urges to swipe the film of Crimson Glory lipstick from her mouth and to pick at her hair. Rosemary had given up on pin curls and instead created a Victory Roll by wringing one of her mother's old stockings into a sort of sausage shape, holding it to the base of Dory's skull, then wrapping her hair up and around it and securing the mess with a nest of bobby pins. Dory thought she looked as if somebody'd stuck a kielbasa to the back of her head.

She turned to Rosemary. "Let's get some punch."

The punch bowl was presided over by Vincent Morello's mother, who beamed at the girls as she dipped into the garish red liquid with a ladle. "Don't you both look lovely!"

Dory and Rosemary chorused their thanks.

Mrs. Morello handed over the cups, then cocked her head and looked at Dory out of the side of her eye. "Now, Doris, are you going to dance with my Vincent?"

Dory, mid-sip, choked on her punch.

The cloying drink shot straight up her nose, and she hacked and wheezed while Rosemary thwacked her on the back. Dory set down the cup and wiped her streaming eyes on her sleeve—well, Rosemary's sleeve—as the fit subsided, grateful, in a way, that the punch in her nose had saved her from having to answer Mrs. Morello's question.

But the question, it seemed, was going to be answered anyhow, as Vincent himself approached from the boys' wall, his jaw set in a determined grimace.

"Jeez Louise," Dory whispered.

Rosemary bit her thumbnail. "He's gonna ask you."

"What should I do?" Dory asked under her breath. She made the mistake of turning to look at Mrs. Morello, who raised her eyebrows in an expression of desperate anticipation.

"Dance with him," Rosemary whispered.

"Jeez Louise," Dory said again.

Vincent greeted them with a wave. "Hi, Rosemary. Hi, Dory."

"Hi, Vincent," Rosemary said.

Dory sniffled.

Vincent fumbled in his pocket and handed her a neatly pressed cotton handkerchief.

"Thanks." Dory blew her nose as delicately as she could. "I kind of choked on my punch."

"I saw." Vincent cleared his throat.

He didn't look at Dory. Dory didn't look at him. A deafening silence hung between them.

Vincent broke first. "Fun dance," he said.

"Yeah," Rosemary said. "Fun dance."

Dory wholeheartedly disagreed, but she nodded anyhow. She couldn't hear much other than her own pulse in her ears, but she recognized that Glenn Miller had stopped and now Kay Kyser was singing "Who Wouldn't Love You."

Vincent shoved his hands into his pockets and looked at Dory. "So...um..."

Aw heck, Dory thought. *He's really going to ask me.*

"Do you want to dance, Dory?"

Dory did not want to dance. Not even a little bit. And even if she had wanted to—which she did not—there was nobody else on the dance floor, which meant that she and Vincent would be out there alone in front of the whole sixth grade. Also, "Who Wouldn't Love You" was an awful song.

Her neck itched terribly.

But there was Vincent, his hands deep in his pockets, his eyes pleading. Dory thought about all the times he had offered to carry her books and help her clap erasers and trade his jam sandwich for her liverwurst and how, if you're going to dance with somebody for the first time ever in your whole life, you should probably do it with a person who is kind.

"Sure," she said.

Vincent's eyes went wide. "Really?"

"Yep."

"Great." Vincent's voice broke.

Rosemary cleared her throat. "I'm just going to . . . um . . ." Apparently, Rosemary didn't really have anything planned, because her voice trailed off as she retreated toward the girls' wall.

Dory looked at Vincent. "So should we just . . . start dancing right here?"

Vincent lowered his voice and leaned closer. "Actually, could we maybe move to the other side of the room? Over by the doors?" He gestured toward the punch table. "Away from, you know, my ma?"

Dory glanced at Mrs. Morello, who was smiling eagerly at them. "Yeah. Let's move." She followed Vincent to the far wall as Kay Kyser warbled on. She balled up Vincent's handkerchief—Vincent's wet handkerchief, now—and slipped it into the sleeve of her borrowed dress. Lack of pockets was one more reason, she thought, why dresses made no sense.

Vincent chose the most out-of-the-way spot on the dance floor, but since the two of them really were the only ones out there, that wasn't saying much. Dory felt the heat of a hundred pairs of eyes on her. Her skin felt like it was on fire. She took a deep breath, then stretched her arms out as far as they'd reach, and placed her hands on Vincent's shoulders, suddenly aware of just how sweaty her palms were. Vincent gave a shaky smile and positioned his hands on her scrawny hips. Even through the crinoline, she could feel that his hands were every bit as sweaty as hers. The two of them shuffled their feet in time to the music.

Which Dory supposed must be dancing.

Kay kept on crooning.

"This is a dopey song," Vincent said.

"Uh-huh."

"I should have waited for a good one to ask you. Like maybe 'Chattanooga Choo Choo.'"

"Yeah. That would have been better."

"Sorry."

"No, it's fine." Dory looked over his shoulder to find that at least five or six other couples had followed them onto the dance floor. Ronald DeMarco and Rosemary were among them. She gestured with her chin. "I think we started something."

Vincent stole a glance. "Looks like it."

The two of them were silent for a whole verse.

It was every bit as awkward as it sounds.

"Any word from your pop?" Vincent said at last.

"Yeah. Week before last. You?"

Vincent shook his head. "It's been a month or so."

Dory stepped on his foot.

Vincent winced.

"Sorry."

"Oh, I hardly felt it." He took one hand off Dory's waist for a moment to pull on the collar of his shirt. "How come you took down your pop's flag?"

Dory startled at the idea that Vincent had noticed the flag's removal. The idea that Vincent looked at her apartment window when he passed. It made sense that he could see it, him living just down the street and all, but still.

She shook the idea from her mind. "Our downstairs neighbor thought we oughta get to know the new landlord before we let on that Pop's away."

"Oh." Vincent nodded. "Makes sense. So have you met him yet?"

"Yeah."

She told Vincent about the matzo ball soup incident.

He shook his head, chuckling. "Yikes."

The song changed. Now it was Bing Crosby and Trudy Erwin singing "People Will Say We're in Love." Which was a whole lot more than Dory could handle.

She stopped swaying. Removed her hands from Vincent's shoulders. Resisted the temptation to wipe them on Rosemary's dress. "Well, thanks, Vincent."

"Oh, gee, Dory. Thank *you!*" His voice broke again. The sound of it hung in the air between them. They stood there staring at each other for what felt like about an hour and a half.

"I don't know how long I'm gonna last," Dory said. "Rosemary put a million bobby pins in my hair and I'm itching to take them out."

"Yeah." Vincent pulled on the knot of his tie. "Ma tied this so tight I can hardly breathe."

Dory grimaced. "Anyhow, thanks again."

Vincent gave a pink-cheeked grin. "I think you're swell, Dory."

Dory didn't think it was possible for her neck to get any itchier, but she grinned back at him anyhow. She decided she was glad she'd said yes when Vincent asked her to dance. Decided that Vincent was the sort of boy who deserved to have girls say yes when he asked them to dance.

Heading back to the girls' wall, she felt in the sleeve of Rosemary's dress for his handkerchief and wondered whether she ought to have given it back. Was a person supposed to give back a handkerchief once it had snot in it? She supposed not.

She watched Rosemary and Ronald sway in time to Bing and Trudy's duet and put all questions of handkerchief etiquette out of her head.

It was time to focus on the reason she'd come to the dance in the first place.

Leaving the dance.

So she could get to the dumbwaiter.

UNTIL
NOW

Caputo's was still busy when Dory arrived—so busy that she wasn't sure anybody even heard the jangling of the bell above the door.

But Mr. Caputo approached from the bar as she entered. "Bambina! What are you doing here? It's Friday!" He took both her hands and lifted her arms, looked her up and down. "You're fancy tonight! You okay? What's the matter?"

"Oh, nothing's the matter, Mr. Caputo." Dory was prepared. "Only, can I please use your bathroom? I'm on my way home from a school dance and I've really gotta go."

Mr. Caputo released her and stepped back to let her pass, oblivious to the fact that there was absolutely no route between school and home that would take her near his restaurant. "Of course! Of course!" he shouted. "You know where it is, bambina!"

As Mr. Caputo went back to the bar and started

inspecting glasses for spots, Dory walked briskly and purposefully to the stairs in the back hall. Then, out of sight, she ran, taking the steps three at a time until she reached the second floor.

Disappearing, as it turned out, was easy.

At the top of the staircase, above the spot where Dory had found the dumbwaiter entrance below, she could see a door that looked just the same. Same worn wood. Same rusted hinges and propeller latch. In front of it were wooden crates of Coca-Cola piled one on top of the other. She ran her fingers over the door. The dumbwaiter was in there, for sure. It was only a question of waiting until Caputo's was empty.

She retrieved Pop's flashlight from her schoolbag. It had a pleasant sort of weight to it. Solid and reassuring. It made her think of Pop's big, weathered hands using it to replace a blown fuse or to light their way home during the dimout. She turned it on and swung it around, performing reconnaissance.

The center of the room was taken up primarily by broken furniture. Some chairs and tables with missing legs. One chair with no legs at all. A broom and dustpan, a wastepaper basket with an old toilet brush in it. Mismatched shelving units sagged under the weight of their loads: dishes, pots and pans, piles of neatly folded napkins, a stack of order pads. Other shelves were full of food. Cans of tomatoes—enough tomatoes, Dory thought, for Mr. Caputo to make about a billion gallons of spaghetti sauce. Sacks of flour. Sacks of potatoes. Olive oil. Coffee beans. Jars of peaches. Powdered milk. Condensed milk. Gelatin. Something mysterious called celery salt.

The second-floor storage area was a perfect place to hide and wait.

Dory removed the bobby pins from her hair. She counted as she went, astounded to find there were thirty-four of them in there. Which seemed like an absolutely unreasonable number of bobby pins. She extracted Mrs. Manzetti's stocking and stuffed it into the front pocket of her schoolbag along with the pins, then changed clothes so she wouldn't muss Rosemary's dress. Getting out of the tight collar and starchy bodice was a relief. She found Vincent's handkerchief in the left sleeve and shoved that into her bag as well.

Comfortable at last, Dory wedged herself into a corner behind the shelves of pots and pans. She hugged her knees to her chest, leaned her head against the brick wall, and waited.

Down below, she heard forks scraping against plates, glasses clinking, bawdy singing, raucous laughter. She heard shattering glass and then—for a few alarming moments, a *clump-clump-clump*-ing up the stairs. Holding her breath, she peeked through the pots and pans. Mr. Caputo appeared, muttering something in Italian as he retrieved the broom and dustpan. A few minutes later, he was back to replace them, still muttering. Dory only started breathing again once she heard him shouting at a busboy downstairs.

For the next half hour or so, the bell over the door

jangled every few minutes, each jangle emptying Caputo's a little bit more. And then there was no more jangling. No more shouting. No more laughter and no more footsteps. The place was quiet.

Dory got up and checked the window. And there was Mr. Caputo, rolling in the awning. She chewed on her thumbnail, her heart thumping as she watched him pocket his keys and shuffle along South Street until he was out of sight.

Now was her time.

She set the flashlight on a table to give herself more light to work by. If she flipped a light switch, a passerby might notice. The fish market and its surrounds were practically a ghost town at this hour, but still. Dory moved the crates of Coca-Cola one at a time. Only enough to get to the dumbwaiter.

She took a deep breath and approached the door.

Just like downstairs, the knob was crusted with rust. Dory gripped it with her thumb and index finger and turned. It didn't budge. She planted her feet for better leverage. Again, nothing. Frustration flared in her nostrils. No way had she gone through all of this to be thwarted by some rust. She'd put on lipstick, for heaven's sake.

There had to be something she could use to get the thing to turn. Jarred peaches were no use, certainly. She didn't imagine celery salt would do the trick. She scanned the rows of shelves until she found a sort of double-sided hammer with metal points on both faces.

"Yikes," she whispered. "It's some kind of a murder weapon."

(It was a meat tenderizer, but Dory didn't know anything about exotic kitchen utensils.)

She carried it to the dumbwaiter, took another deep breath, and tapped the knob on its right side.

It didn't move, but some rust flaked off and fell to the floor.

Three taps, a little harder now. The knob definitely shifted.

Two more taps. And the closure gave way.

Her heart pounding, Dory dropped the mallet, gripped the door's edge, and pulled. The hinges shrieked. And the thing opened.

Holy mackerel. There it was.

The dumbwaiter.

Dory inched forward with the flashlight for a better look. She hardly dared breathe, half expecting something to jump out at her. In *Frankenstein Meets the Wolf Man*, Lon Chaney would have thought an elevator shaft was a perfect place to lie in wait for his next victim.

Her palms sweating—almost as much as they had when she was dancing with Vincent—Dory trained the flashlight's beam on the century-old hand elevator and gave a low whistle.

"It's nothing like the one in the Empire State Building, that's for sure," she whispered.

It was more of a cage than an elevator. Vertical iron slats for side walls, crisscrossed ones for the floor. Furred with the dust of years, the only thing in it was a pair of heavy ropes hanging through the bars at the top.

Gripping the flashlight's hilt like some sort of lifeline to Pop, Dory held on to the wall with one hand and leaned into the cage. Overhead, the dumbwaiter's ropes extended up and up and up, beyond the space illuminated by the flashlight's beam. Airless and black and still, the only sound was a sort of distant scratching, as if the opening of the dumbwaiter door had roused the rats that had claimed the building's walls decades ago. Dory shivered.

She touched one of the hemp ropes. It was just like those that tethered the skiffs to the dock in the East River below, only a billion years older. Dory had no idea how a dumbwaiter worked, but she figured one of the ropes must pull the thing up and the other must let it down again. She patted the rope harder, releasing a shadow of dust and a thin whine from the darkness above. The sound of metal on metal, she supposed.

Well, like people said, there was only one way to skin a cat. Or maybe it was more than one way. Whichever it was, Dory thought it an awfully strange expression.

She decided it was best to test the contraption's mettle without actually getting into it. Looking around the storage room, her eyes landed on the potatoes.

"Better them than me," she said. She set the flashlight back on the table and got to work.

The first sack, ten pounds laid gingerly on the dumbwaiter floor, didn't budge the thing a bit. With the second, Dory heard the same iron-ish whine from above, like the hinge of a coffin opening. But still no movement. Promising. Sacks three through six yielded the same high-pitched whine. Dory paused. Shone the flashlight up into the shaft again. Saw nothing but the haze of dust illuminated by the beam. The seventh sack produced a metallic cough from above, but the cage held steady. And the addition of sack eight—eighty pounds of spuds in all, or approximately the weight of one Dory—resulted in a drop of only an inch or two.

Which was probably fine, right?

Dory decided it was fine.

The next question was whether the ropes would budge the thing.

Still standing outside the cage, she chose the closer rope and gave it a determined tug. A shower of dust and rusted bits of metal rained down on the potatoes, but nothing else moved. She tugged harder. Still nothing. She spit on her hands and threw all her weight onto the rope. There was a grating squeal from the shaft above, and the dumbwaiter moved upward about six inches.

Holy moly.

Dory grinned so wide the sides of her mouth hurt.

She tried the other rope, and, sure enough, as long as she pulled on it with all her might, that one lowered the cage back down. The thing worked. Lifting out the sacks of potatoes and replacing them where she'd found them, she gathered her flashlight and schoolbag, setting the light upright in the open bag to illuminate the air above her.

She stepped inside the dumbwaiter without giving it a second thought.

Well, all right. She did give it a second thought.

Four second thoughts, to be precise. Four fears. The things Dory feared were:

1. Falling. Obviously.
2. Getting stuck. Yikes. Worse than falling.
3. Finding dead bodies up there. Dory thought about this for only a moment before deciding it was definitely worse than items 1 and 2.
4. Finding nothing.

In her secret heart, Dory thought that item 4 really was the worst possible thing. What if she got up there to find empty rooms? The notion was so heartbreaking, it put the idea of dead bodies out of her mind entirely.

She pulled on the rope. Hung on it, in fact, until her fanny touched the cage's floor. The dumbwaiter lurched upward about eight or ten inches, and a menace of furry dust filtered into the cage. Dory shook her head to get it out of her hair and hung on the rope again. Another ten inches, another plume of dust, another shake of the head. Again. Then again.

Pausing to stretch her fingers, she retrieved the light from her bag and swung it right and left. Above her, she could just see the outline of a door about four feet away. Her heart fluttered. She repositioned Pop's flashlight in her bag and pulled on the rope again. Again. Again. Dust and grime continued to cascade from the innards of the building, landing on her face like snow. She sneezed. Once. Twice. Three times. Each sneeze thundered. The dumbwaiter swayed like a skiff on a choppy sea.

"Bless me," Dory said aloud. She rubbed at her nose with her sleeve, which came away smeared with black. Even in the dim light of the flashlight's beam, she could see the dirt. Fish was going to kill her.

(To be clear: Of all the reasons Fish might have had to kill Dory that night, getting her blouse dirty was probably not at the top of the list.)

By now, she could see the lower hinge of the third-floor door. She closed her eyes and heaved on the rope four more times, grunting "Treasure" with every pull.

And suddenly, there she was.

On the dumbwaiter side of the third-floor door, Dory saw the same sort of propeller-style closure as below. The inner and outer hardware turned as one, it seemed, allowing the doors to be latched and unlatched from either side. Dory reached for the propeller. Jeez Louise, she should have stuck that murder mallet in her school-bag. What if this one was rusted shut, too?

But it wasn't. It turned with relative ease, and with a little push, the door swung forward.

Her hands shaking, Dory fumbled the flashlight out of her bag and shone it around Caputo's third floor, unseen for years and years and years.

Until now.

WHAT
POSSIBLE
TREASURE

Her pulse clunking in her ears, Dory peered out of the dumbwaiter.

If there were dead bodies, would they smell? She supposed not. If they'd been dead twenty or more years, they'd be done rotting by now, right? So they'd be more skeletons than bodies. That thought wasn't especially comforting.

Dory ventured one toe out of the dumbwaiter, testing the floor to make sure it would hold. Her foot met solid wood, and she willed the rest of herself out of the cage and into...

Well, what was it, exactly?

To her right, the flashlight's beam landed on an exposed brick wall with two large windows, boarded on the outside. Sconces on either side of the windows held the stubs of candles in blackened glass covers. In the middle was a piano, peeling and decrepit. Dory went to it on tiptoe and extended a tentative finger toward one of the keys, releasing a tinny note. At the sound, she heard a skittering and swung Pop's flashlight toward it, catching what looked like the end of a rat's tail disappearing into the darkness.

She froze, picturing an army of rodents surging from under the piano, or a flurry of vampire bats coming out of the rafters. She directed the flashlight at the ceiling. Just a web of cracked and peeling plaster, a few exposed beams.

"It was only one rat," she whispered.

(Which was ridiculous, of course. There is never only one rat.)

To her left was a series of doors, all closed. The nearest bore a worn brass plate engraved with the number 1. In front of her was a wooden counter, and behind that an odd sort of wall with a grid of recessed cubbyholes. The center of the grid held a rack of pegs, and on each peg was a numbered key.

It was a hotel.

That's all it was. Just an old hotel.

Dory swallowed a glob of disappointment.

What possible treasure could there be in an old hotel?

She lowered her flashlight. Sighed. Gritted her teeth. Willed herself to think positive.

Maybe a mobster had stayed here. Al Capone, maybe? Would he have been a guest at a place like this?

What about Captain Kidd? When was Captain Kidd

around, again? And who was that other pirate Pike had told her about? The one who got hung—hanged—out on Libby's island? Did pirates even stay in hotels? Dory wasn't sure they did. She wished she'd paid better attention to Pike. Or spent more time at the library.

She set her jaw and squared her shoulders.

There had to be something worthwhile in this crumbling old place. There just had to be.

And she had the rest of the night to find it.

*

She inspected the cubbies first. All but one was empty unless you counted the half inch of dust. Which Dory did not. From the center cubby on the bottom row, she pulled an envelope, still sealed. The writing on the front was faded but legible in the flashlight's beam. The penmanship, Dory noted, would have earned excellent marks for its perfectly even loops. Its sender was M. Whetstone, 525 Elm Street, Schenectady, New York, and the recipient was one Chester C. Howell, The South Street Hotel, South Street, New York.

The South Street Hotel. Dory sniffed. Not very imaginative.

When she slipped her finger under the envelope's flap, the yellowed paper fell away easily. Perhaps she ought not to be reading somebody else's mail, but this letter must be so old, Dory supposed, that whatever M. Whetstone had written didn't matter much anymore. She slid it out, a single sheet, folded in neat thirds and dated October 15, 1889.

Dory gave a low whistle. Over fifty years ago, that was. She read the elegant scrawl:

My Dear Chester,
I hope your travels were comfortable, that you've safely arrived at your hotel, and that this letter finds its way to you.

(Dory guessed she knew how that had worked out).

I do so regret the way we parted. Words spoken in anger leave the most painful of wounds. I can only hope that those I inflicted upon you were not mortal.

(Yikes. That seemed a little over the top.)

Should your proposal of marriage still stand, I want you to know that I accept. In no uncertain terms, I accept.

(Uh-oh.)

Yours ever,
Mae

Chester and Mae were probably dead by now, but Dory felt a pang, hoping that somehow they'd been reunited and had a good laugh about whatever it was Mae had said in anger. She hoped they'd gotten married and settled down in Schenectady and had about ten kids and a hundred grandkids. She slipped the letter back into its slot.

What to investigate next? There were shelves under the counter—the hotel's reception desk, Dory supposed—bearing an assortment of uselessness. Bottles, still half-full of some sort of liquor. A stack of rotting newspapers. A pile of hotel flyers. Someone's spectacles. A chipped sugar bowl. A decaying spool of black thread. On the countertop was a dusty old cash register.

A cash register.

Cash was just as good as pirate treasure.

Dory hit one of the buttons. Nothing happened. She tried another one. Still nothing.

There was a crank on the contraption's right-hand side. When she turned it, the drawer released with a reluctant ping.

Inside was a single coin. Dory rubbed it with her thumb. UNITED STATES OF AMERICA, it said, 1886. She turned it over. *One dime.* Ten cents. Her eyes burning at the insult of it, Dory pocketed the miserable coin and closed the cash drawer with a bang.

She looked next at the rack of keys, still neat on their pegs after all these years. Gathering them one by one, she dropped them into her schoolbag.

All but the key for the first door. Room 1. That seemed as good a place to start as any.

The lock opened with a satisfying clunk, and the door swung inward with a haunted-house sort of creak. Other than that, the place was utterly silent. Dory cleared her throat. If a vampire were in there, waiting to drink her blood, she'd be able to hear footsteps or something, wouldn't she? Even a ghost would make some sort of *whooo*-ing sound, right? She stepped inside.

There was a chest of drawers, a desk and chair, a wardrobe, a mirror, and a narrow wrought-iron bed neatly made. The patchwork quilt was frosted with dust. She checked the drawers. All empty. Inside the wardrobe, a single black cloak had been left to rot. A useless black cloak.

Dory moved on.

Room 2 was laid out identically. Same mirror. Same quilt. Same desk. Same wardrobe, though in this one no useless cloak.

Room 3 was similarly empty. Or so Dory thought, until she opened the wardrobe and a small glass ball—a lone marble, she supposed—fell out and landed on her foot. It rolled to the other side of the room, coming to rest against the desk chair. Dory retrieved it and turned it over in her hand. She shone the flashlight's beam on it for a better look.

It looked back at her.

She dropped it as quickly as she'd picked it up.

It was a glass eyeball.

Dory cringed as the thing rolled toward the door in a jiggedy-jaggedy way. Not like a marble would roll but, well, like an eye would—until it stopped at the doorjamb.

She crossed the room and picked it up again. It was greenish-blue with flecks of gold. It was hideous and marvelous and terrifying. It had once been inside somebody's head.

The glorious monstrosity deserved to be someplace better than the third shelf down in a musty old wardrobe. Stepping into the lobby, Dory looked around and settled on the molding around the door to room 3. It was deep enough to hold the glass orb. She balanced the eye in the top middle, where it stared out at the lobby. Keeping an eye on things, as it were.

Dory offered the eyeball a solemn salute before peeking into the last two rooms at the end of the hall. An institutional space with several large metal tubs and a tiny lavatory with a sink and a toilet. The sort that flushed with a chain. Dory eyed it curiously, then reached for the handle and gave it a tentative pull. The tank coughed and sputtered and clanked, and for a horrifying second she pictured the thing exploding. Among the many dangers she'd imagined in this escapade, the risk of toilet explosion had never occurred to her. But the bowl merely filled with rust-colored water, then drained peacefully.

Dory returned to the dumbwaiter and hauled herself up to the next level.

Surely that's where the treasure would be.

On the fourth floor, she found the same boarded windows to her right. Between them was a wardrobe with folded linens inside. A rusted sewing machine—the pedal sort, still threaded—languished in a corner. On the far wall was a chess table, its pieces mid-game as if the players had simply tired of it and gone to bed, agreeing to pick up where they'd left off the next day. Behind it, the plaster had fallen away in spots, leaving gaping holes that exposed the innards of the crumbling hotel.

She set to exploring the bedrooms, each more useless than the last. Rusted bed frames. Grime-filmed mirrors. Wardrobes, empty but for a discarded sock here and there.

Room 6 was only a little more promising. Stashed in the desk drawer was a framed photograph of a lady in a long dark dress. She was smiling. Which was unusual, Dory thought. Old-timey people didn't often smile in photographs. Yet here was this one, grinning out at her from the tarnished silver.

Silver. Silver was a sort of treasure, wasn't it?

She picked at the frame with her thumbnail and watched flakes peel away.

Silver paint. No sort of treasure at all.

Setting the pointless picture back in the drawer, Dory noticed a scrap of paper. It was maybe a third of a page, torn from a book, it seemed. Only a few lines were visible:

Why, who makes much of a miracle?
As to me I know of nothing else but miracles,
Whether I walk the streets of Manhattan,
Or dart my sight over the roofs of houses toward the sky,

The poem ended mid-sentence. And it didn't even rhyme, for Pete's sake.

But scrawled at the top were three words: *My Beloved Mae.*

Dory swallowed hard. *Beloved.* Just like in Pop's letters.

That must be Chester's Mae smiling out at her from the photograph. Mae, who had accepted Chester's proposal of marriage in her letter. And Chester, who had never gotten it. This was Chester's room.

Dory sat herself down in the desk chair, the flashlight in one hand, the scrap of poem in the other. She thought about how important it was, being beloved. How important it was, beloving somebody. She retrieved Mae and tucked her inside her schoolbag.

The poem she returned to the desk.

Dory Byrne didn't make much of miracles.

✳

The fifth floor was laid out backward to the ones below. There was a single door on her right, while the rest of the space was an open room, empty but for an old-fashioned potbellied stove against the far wall, a handful of mismatched chairs, and two large covered tables. Dory lifted the sheets draped over them, revealing a card table with a pack of cards fanned in its center, and a billiard table. With billiard balls and everything. And a rack of cue sticks on the wall behind it.

Other than that, there was just one room on the fifth floor.

She shone the flashlight on the door.

Room 7. The very last one. She sighed.

By now, Dory had pretty much resigned herself to the fact that there was no treasure.

But can a person ever completely resign herself to such a thing? When there is only one room left to explore, could you blame a person for holding on to just a smidge of hope that this last room will be the place?

"Please," Dory whispered. "Let this last room be the place."

She opened the door and looked around in the shifting glow of the flashlight. Took a long, shuddering breath.

It was a bedroom. Larger, but otherwise not so different from the others.

She bit her lip. "It's just another room."

Hot tears welled in the corners of her eyes. She'd wanted something magnificent. Pirate treasure. Gold bars hidden away by bank robbers. Even a nice collection of baseball cards would have been better than this old place. Hugging herself against the chill of disappointment in her rib cage, she swung the flashlight around halfheartedly.

Two windows, boarded up like all the others, only with seats built into the wall beneath them. A large bed and a bedside table. A rolltop desk. Candle sconces on the walls.

A trio of chairs huddled in the corner, white sheets covering each of them, turning them into a haunt of ghosts. Dory shivered in spite of herself.

There were two wardrobes. Twins, both intricately carved with leaves and vines, they flanked the doorway as if standing guard. Dory opened the one on the left and shone the light inside to find three coat hangers on the rod and a gray mitten abandoned on a low shelf. She gave the leg of the wardrobe a kick, furious at its useless contents.

The one on the right held even less. It was entirely empty, as far as Dory could see.

Before the flashlight died.

She gasped. Blinked at the sudden darkness.

There is never a particularly convenient time for a flashlight to die, but there were four reasons that this time was especially problematic:

1. Being in an abandoned hotel in the middle of the night. Obviously.
2. The only way out—as you surely recall—was through the dumbwaiter. Which would be difficult and terrifying to use in utter darkness.
3. Dory had recently been thinking about ghosts.

Items 1 through 3 were obvious. You could have guessed them. You probably did guess them.

Item 4 is different. You couldn't possibly guess it. Not if you were given a hundred million guesses. Not even if you are a smarty-pants.

Item 4 was the following: Dory's flashlight died before she noticed the diamond.

Yes. The diamond.

Inside the wardrobe, on the second shelf from the top, in the very back corner, was a single diamond earring. A fantastic one. An enormous one. Had Pop's flashlight held out just a little bit longer, perhaps Dory would have shone it just so and would have caught the flash of brilliance when the beam reflected off the icy stone. Perhaps she would have picked it up between her thumb and forefinger, inspected it closely, wondered if it was real (it was), and—if so—how somebody could have left such a thing behind (it was an accident).

None of this happened.

Because Pop's flashlight died.

So there the diamond stayed. On the second shelf from the top, inside the wardrobe on the right side of the door to room 7. On the fifth floor of the old hotel.

The old hotel that, as far as Dory Byrne knew, did not contain any treasure whatsoever.

WHAT WE MIGHT
CALL A DOWNWARD
SPIRAL

D ory did not cry.
   She thought about crying. Really, she thought
about it quite seriously. She thought about the terrifying
nature of darkness, and about how much flashlight batteries cost. She thought about the decisions made by New York
City's pirates—the fact that they had apparently never once
considered hiding their booty in an East River hotel—and
what a tragedy this was for both herself and the city at
large. But she resisted the temptation to cry. She did this by
biting her tongue until she could almost taste blood.

   Having no idea what time it was, Dory knew only that
if she spent the rest of the night alone in the leaden darkness of the old hotel, she'd go batty and end up like the
man who hung around the Canal Street subway station
shouting about the devil and President Roosevelt. She
had to get out, and she had to get out now.

Shutting her eyes tight (seeing-wise, eyes open or eyes closed didn't make much difference at the moment), Dory felt her way to the door of room 7. She knew she'd left her schoolbag on the floor as she'd come in, and she felt with her toe until she found it. Stowing the useless flashlight, she slung the bag over her chest crosswise. She blinked again and again, willing her eyes to adjust, but the boarded windows left the old hotel as black as pitch.

She set her teeth determinedly. In her mind's eye, she conjured a picture of the billiard room. The table was maybe six or eight paces from room 7, and it was roughly in front of the dumbwaiter. It followed that, if she could make it to the billiard table, she only needed to turn left and she'd find her way out.

Stretching her hands in front of her, Dory shuffled forward, trying hard to ignore the thought that there might be rats staring at her from the darkness. (There were.)

One step. Two steps. Three. She thought about the ghosts in room 7 and wondered whether they might have followed her. (They hadn't. They were chairs.)

Five steps. Six. Seven. Dory's hip hit something solid, and she lowered her hand to feel the edge of the billiard table. She made her way to the corner pocket, then to the center on the dumbwaiter side. Eyes still clamped shut, she put the center pocket to her back and slid her feet forward again.

How many paces was it from the billiard table to the dumbwaiter? Eight? Maybe ten? Dory started counting steps out loud as she went but found that the sound of her own trembling voice only made things worse. She bit down on her tongue again to stop the panic.

Her hand met the wall. She made her way to the right, feeling along the gritty bricks, shuffling her feet in the darkness. Should she have gone left instead? No. Right felt right.

And it was. She reached what felt like an edge.

Her heart in her throat, Dory extended a hand until she felt cold iron. The dumbwaiter.

She breathed a sigh of relief. Then wondered why in the name of all that was holy she would feel something as ridiculous as relief. She still had to climb into the creaking cage and haul herself down three floors in inky darkness.

Edging her right foot forward, Dory felt for the spot where the dumbwaiter met the floor. There it was. A slight depression. She twined her fingers around one of the contraption's iron bars and took a step. The dumbwaiter gave a bit with her weight, and her heart hammered in her chest.

"I tested this with potatoes," she said out loud. Her voice still quavered alarmingly.

Groping in the darkness, Dory's hands met the bristly surface of the ropes. It was the one on the right that would lower the cage, wasn't it? She thought so. Gripping it with sweaty fingers, she hung on it with all of her seventy-nine pounds. There was a whimper from the winch, and a familiar storm of dust and corroded iron from above. She felt the patter of it on her face but heaved on the rope again, shaking off the debris that rained down on her.

After five pulls, she extended a hand to see whether she'd reached the fourth-floor landing yet. Her fingers met only the inside of the dumbwaiter shaft. Two more pulls. Still just bricks. Three more, and at last Dory held out her hand to feel the open air of the fourth floor. Pop always got sore at her for leaving doors open, but at the moment she was glad she hadn't yet broken the habit. She paused to catch her breath, then hung on the rope again.

Down and down and down she went, counting each pull. An even ten pulls brought her to the opening for the third floor. "One more floor to go," she whispered.

Her palms were sore from the rough hemp, but as she hauled herself down to the second floor, her terror gave way to pride. She'd done it: felt her way in the dark, past the ghosts and the rats and the peril—and there she was in Caputo's storage room again. She knew she'd arrived because she could see it. The moon shone bright through the windows, illuminating the canned tomatoes and the toilet brush and the crates of Coca-Cola.

The sight of the moon through the filmy glass suggested that there must be at least a couple of hours of night left. She couldn't go home yet, or she'd have a lot of explaining to do.

Dory wiped the sweat from her forehead. Sneaking into Caputo's was something she'd put a lot of thought into. As for sneaking out? She was less prepared. She couldn't just unlock the door and leave, because there would be no way for her to lock it behind her. Poor Mr. Caputo would arrive on Monday and wonder whether he had either been robbed or forgotten to lock it himself. Mr. Caputo was swell. It would be a shame to make him think he was going bananas.

She closed the dumbwaiter door. Put the crates of Coca-Cola back in place. Made her way down to the restaurant below. It felt entirely different in the stillness of the wee hours. Chairs were upturned on tables, the menu board wiped blank. The whole place had an ammonia-smelling sort of cleanliness to it.

Dory checked the front windows. All four were carefully latched. Perhaps the kitchen? She made her way through the swinging doors, past a long counter crisscrossed with knife marks. At the very back, a heavy door was securely padlocked. But next to that was a battery of sinks under a single small window whose lock, Dory found, hung on only one hinge.

Making it of little use, as locks go.

Raising herself onto the rim of one of the sinks, Dory opened the window with a grunt and heaved her schoolbag into Caputo's back alley so that she could slide through unencumbered. Only then did she look down to find that her bag had landed in a large metal garbage bin beneath the window. A garbage bin that was full of the leavings of last night's dinner service. Fish skins. Clamshells. Spent grease from the griddle. All things that—left overnight in a festering heap—come to smell like death itself.

Dory grimaced. Hoisted herself out the window and balanced on the garbage bin, one foot on either side. A scrawny cat watched her from against the alley wall as she juddered the window shut and jumped to the ground. The cat skittered away at the thud, then paused at the end of the alley to regard her with cool detachment. As cats do.

Dory held her breath and retrieved her bag from the bin, picking a fish head off the strap.

"Disgusting," she whispered.

The cat did not appear to agree. In fact, he looked like he had spent his whole life hoping for a fish head just like this one.

Dory sniffed. "At least one of us oughta get something good out of this place." She threw the head to the cat, who polished it off in a few eager bites, then looked at her expectantly, as if hoping for more. She bent to scratch between his ears. "You're cute and all, but I'm not about to reach into the garbage again for you. Besides," she said, "I've got to go meet a friend."

The cat cocked his head at her.

And Dory walked south. Toward the Castle.

* * *

Out in the harbor, the first fingers of daylight were just creeping over the horizon. It was light enough that, even without Pop's binoculars, Libby was visible out there on her island. Dory stood on the Castle wall, trying to swallow the gobbet of disappointment lodged in her throat.

"It was useless, Libby. Not a speck of treasure."

Libby just stood there, of course, though her right foot was poised—always poised—as if she were about to make a run for it.

"There was nothing."

Still, the Green Goddess was silent out there in her watery kingdom.

"Unless you count a picture frame and a puny little dime," Dory groused, glaring at Libby. She kicked at a piece of debris, sending it bouncing toward the harbor.

Libby had done nothing wrong, of course. But just now Dory wanted someone to blame, because just now Dory's thoughts were going in what we might call a downward spiral. Disappointment can do that to a person. Especially a person who has already suffered a good deal more disappointment than seems fair.

As the tears fell and the snot bubbled in her nose, Dory's despondency at the lack of pirate treasure or anything else of any merit in the old hotel led her to envision a grim and unhappy future. It went something like this:

1. Pop would never come home.
2. Fish would have to look after her and Pike forever and ever, which would mean he wouldn't find a girl and get married because who'd marry a boy who had to drag his brother and sister along behind him wherever he went? Done in by loneliness, Fish would turn to the bottle and end up sleeping under the Brooklyn Bridge.
3. Pike—who, understandably, didn't want to sleep under the Brooklyn Bridge—would run away, his most treasured possessions tied

in a bundle on the end of a stick slung over his shoulder. As he hopped a westbound boxcar, his foot would slip, and he'd be crushed to a pulp beneath the train's wheels.

4. Dory would be left to fend for herself. She'd drop out of school in the eighth grade and get a job mopping the bathrooms in Grand Central. She'd save up to pay for a headstone for Pike. She'd visit Fish under the bridge when she could.

Well, now she was just feeling sorry for herself.

It was a mild night, but the adrenaline that lingered in her veins after her escape from the old hotel had her shivering. She wrapped her arms around her rib cage and gazed out at the water until something moving in the rubble below caught her eye. She squinted.

The cat, it seemed, had followed her.

Dory grinned in spite of herself. She bent low, holding out her arms for the creature, who leaped from one stone to another and into her waiting hands. She sat down on the ramparts and cradled the thing in her lap. He was nothing but skin and bones—rather like Dory herself—but somewhere beneath that skin and those bones, he was also warmth and determination and fierce affection. Somewhere beneath that skin and those bones, he needed saving.

Also rather like Dory herself.

And in the handful of moments it took for it to beat

only five or six times, Dory Byrne's heart, so broken with disappointment and yearning, resolved that it wanted this scrawny and very likely flea-bitten cat. Wanted to be the one to save him.

She stroked him from ears to tail, his contented purring warming her to her bones.

She let him lick her fingers with his sandpaper tongue.

She sat and figured what she'd have to say to Fish to convince him they needed a pet.

Twisting her neck to glance back at the great city behind her, Dory sighed. Thought about the wasted night. The useless old hotel.

She turned back to the water and looked toward Libby. Stroked the cat's bony ribs.

"Well. So."

Dory sniffled.

"Maybe not completely useless."

*

She walked home—the cat nestled on top of Rosemary's party dress, inside her schoolbag—as the white and slanting sun of early morning wound its way through the maze of the Lower East Side, reflecting off windows here and there, a patchwork of light. It was the first time Dory had ever stayed up all night, though not the first time she'd tried. In the third grade, she'd made it until nearly four in the morning at Cecelia Conti's slumber party, but that was only because Cecelia kept poking her when she started to nod off.

Climbing the fire escape in a heavy-legged daze, she didn't notice Mrs. Kopek at her open window until she snapped the dust out of a doormat and nearly gave Dory a coronary.

She let out a shriek.

"Doris!" Mrs. Kopek shouted. "You scared me!"

"Sorry, Mrs. Kopek." Dory's startled heart slowed.

"What are you doing out so early, child? And how'd you get so filthy?"

Dory stifled a yawn. "I slept over at my friend's house. And I..." She looked down at her clothes. How to explain the filthy part? "I, uh..."

As if he heard her floundering, the cat poked his head out of Dory's schoolbag and greeted her neighbor with a winning grunt. The diversion worked like a charm. A smile erupted from Mrs. Kopek's wrinkles, all questions of filth evaporating.

"Oh!" she cried. "Sweet little puss! Where'd you come from?" Mrs. Kopek reached out and let the cat nuzzle his head against her hand.

Dory thought quickly. "My friend found him."

She thought quickly some more. "But her dad's allergic, so I brought him home with me."

Mrs. Kopek looked at Dory knowingly. "Will your brother let you keep him, do you think?"

Dory bit her lower lip. "I hope so." A tooth-rattling yawn caught her by surprise.

"Child," Mrs. Kopek said. "You look dead on your feet." She draped the mat over the windowsill and turned back toward her apartment. "Give me just a second. I've made paczki and want to give you some."

Paczki. What on earth might paczki be? Mrs. Kopek was forever giving them strange food. Dory knew she should feel grateful, but with things like pickled mushrooms and lard spread on rye toast, that was awfully hard.

Mrs. Kopek returned with a covered dish. "Paczki," she said.

Dory mustered something that looked like a smile.

"Jam doughnuts."

"Oh." Dory's relief was audible. "Thanks, Mrs. Kopek. Thanks a lot." She balanced the dish on her left hip and started up the stairs. "See you later."

"Enjoy that dear little kitty!" Mrs. Kopek said. "And get some sleep!"

Dory clambered toward the third-floor landing, the fire escape clanging. "I will!" she shouted, louder than she should have, given the hour.

Through his apartment window, she saw Mr. Kowalczyk startle at the noise.

"Sorry," she whispered.

Mr. Kowalczyk inclined his head in a sort of a question mark, narrowing his eyes at her until the skin between them puckered in three vertical stitches.

Dory held his questioning gaze for only a moment before she looked away.

The recluse did the same.

LIKE
BELA
LUGOSI

The boys were still asleep.

Which gave Dory some time to collect herself. And after the night's events, there was a lot of collecting to do. She set Mrs. Kopek's paczki on the kitchen table and loosed the cat. "Go ahead and explore," she said, stroking him under the chin. "And when Fish wakes up, be sure to make a good first impression."

The cat appeared confident in his ability to do just that.

Dory tiptoed into the bedroom she shared with Pike. His slow, soft breathing never changed as she emptied her schoolbag onto the floor, shoved its contents—Rosemary's dress, thirty-four bobby pins, Vincent's handkerchief, Pop's dead flashlight, the old hotel's not-treasures—under the bed, and retrieved clean clothes from the chest of drawers. She changed in the living room, then threw her dirty things into the kitchen sink, scrubbed and rubbed and rinsed them, and hung them to dry on the fire escape.

Evidence of the old hotel thus disposed of, Dory reclined on the sofa with a sigh. The cat joined her, curling himself into a ball on her stomach.

"We're going to have to come up with a name for you," she said, his rumbling purr tickling her belly. "We can't just call you *cat*."

Some cats are named for their looks, she thought. *Tabby. Fluffy. Ginger.* But this specimen was none of those things. In fact, if she was going to go by looks, she ought to call him Scraggly, but a name like that wasn't going to win anybody over.

Dory closed her eyes in concentration. And promptly fell asleep.

*

She woke to Pike's shouting.

"It's a cat! It's a cat! It's a cat!" He clapped his hands with gleeful abandon, jumping up and down and firing questions at her in rapid succession. "Whose is he, Dory? *Is* he a he? What's his name?"

The cat stretched and yawned, grunting in indignation at being roused so abruptly.

Dory did the same. She rubbed crust from her eyes, sat up, and adjusted the cat on her lap. "He's a stray, Pike. So he doesn't have a name." *Yet,* she thought. "And yeah, he's a he."

Pike, beaming, joined Dory on the sofa and reached

to nuzzle the creature under his chin. "Can we keep him? Did you ask Fish?"

Dory was about to grouse that Fish wasn't enough of a grown-up to get to decide about cats. That they'd have to write to Pop, if it came to that.

But Fish appeared from his bedroom with a sleep-skewed mop of hair. "Ask Fish what?"

"We've got a cat!" Pike shouted. "Dory got him for us!"

That's it, Pike, Dory thought. *Keep up that level of enthusiasm, and Fish will have to be convinced.*

But as Fish's eyes, still heavy, landed on the cat, it quickly became clear that he wouldn't need much convincing. His face lit up with a wide grin as he came to the sofa and lowered himself next to Pike.

The cat arose, gave a friendly *mew,* and strolled from Dory's knees to Pike's to Fish's, where he turned in a circle and planted himself comfortably, glancing up at Dory as if to say, *How's that for a first impression?*

Fish stroked his back. "Where'd you find him, Dor?"

By the garbage bin in Caputo's back alley was certainly the wrong answer. So Dory went with the same story she'd told Mrs. Kopek, about Rosemary's dad being allergic. "Can we keep him, Fish? Please?"

"Yeah, please, can we?" Pike echoed.

Fish smiled as the cat licked his thumb. "Affectionate little guy," he said. "Kinda looks like one I've seen down by the fish market. Scrounging for food in the alley off Fulton Street."

Dory swallowed. Oh boy.

But Fish, she realized, had hit on something. "Fulton! That's a perfect name!"

Pike took the cat from Fish's lap and draped it over his own. "Fulton," he whispered. "I think that means we're keeping you." He bent and planted a kiss between the cat's ears. "Once you've named something, you've gotta keep it."

Dory looked at Fish, her eyes pleading.

He grinned. "I've always wanted a cat."

Dory grinned back at him. She hated to admit it, but this was one advantage of having a seventeen-year-old brother for a guardian. When it came to pets, seventeen-year-old brothers were apparently quite easy to convince.

Fish squinted at her. "Why are you home so early, Dor?"

"Oh…" Dory had to think for only a second. "Mr. Manzetti was starting to break out in hives, so me and the cat—" She smiled. "Me and Fulton needed to get out of his hair."

This whole lying thing was feeling way too easy.

Dory's stomach groaned, reminding her about the doughnuts on the counter. "Hey!" she said. "Mrs. Kopek gave us breakfast."

Pike grimaced. "What is it?"

Fish's grimace mirrored his brother's. "Does it involve beets?"

Dory snorted. "Nope." She crossed to the kitchen table. "They're jam doughnuts." She retrieved plates and parceled out the paczki, stopping for only a moment to sniff them, just in case. They definitely didn't smell like beets.

Fish switched on the radio and found Vera Lynn singing "The White Cliffs of Dover." He turned it up loud, and the three of them sat at the kitchen table. Fulton took Pop's chair.

Pike chomped on a doughnut, powdered sugar bearding his chin. He grinned at Dory. "Did Mrs. Kopek complain about the bunnies on her feet?"

Dory chuckled. "Not today."

Pike gestured toward Fish. "He got the job, you know."

Dory looked at him. "At the Navy Yard?"

"Yeah," Fish said. "Letter came yesterday. But it's not a job. It's an apprenticeship."

"Still," Pike said. "He's going places. Just like Pop always says."

Dory stifled a yawn and congratulated her brother. She meant it, too.

"So how was the dance?" Fish asked.

"Fine."

"Did you dance?"

"A little." Dory yawned outright. Her body felt leaden. As if she'd been up all night.

Which...well.

Fish raised his eyebrows at her. "A little?"

Dory shrugged.

"With who?" Fish asked.

"Whom," Pike corrected.

A glob of jam oozed out the end of Dory's doughnut and plopped onto her plate. "Vincent."

Fish's eyes went wide. "Vincent Morello?"

"Yeah."

"Irene's brother?"

"Uh-huh."

Fish poked her shoulder with a sugar-sticky finger. "Are you sweet on him?"

"No!" Dory shouted. A little too loud to be believable.

Fish mopped up a puddle of jelly with the end of his doughnut. "Is he sweet on you?"

Dory crossed her arms and sighed. Which was a sort of an answer.

Fish grinned knowingly. "Yikes."

"Gross," Pike said, his mouth full.

Dory gave Fish a long look. "Wait—are you sweet on Irene?"

Fish occupied himself with licking sugar from his fingers. His cheeks bloomed pink.

"You are!" Dory shouted. "You and Irene Morello!"

Fish smiled. "I'm not the one who danced with Vincent last night!"

Pike joined in, singing an off-key playground song about Dory and her *boyfriend* and *k-i-s-s-i-n-g*.

Dory was entirely too exhausted to handle this with dignity. She punched Pike in the shoulder. Harder than she meant to.

Pike inhaled sharply. As the radio blared Bing Crosby, "Swinging on a Star," Dory waited for the wailing she knew was coming. It started from Pike's belly, winding up like an air raid siren until it finally made its way through his windpipe and escaped from his mouth, a long, piercing howl.

Fulton leaped up from Pop's chair and retreated toward the bedrooms.

Dory considered following him.

"Aw, for Pete's sake, Dory." Fish picked Pike up and held him as the shrieking continued. "Why'd you have to go and hit him?" he shouted.

Dory fumed. Exhaustion, last night's disappointment, and now Pike's nonsense were giving her a headache. She stuck her fingers in her ears. "I didn't hit him *that* hard!"

"You did too!" Pike screeched.

"I did not! You're just being a baby!"

They couldn't hear the knocking on the apartment door over the music and the wailing and the shouting.

Until the knocking became pounding. Angry pounding.

Pike's sobs ended abruptly.

Fish set him back on his feet. "Shut off the radio, Dor."

She did. Fish opened the door. It was the new landlord.

He stood in the doorway wearing a stained undershirt and a scowl. "Loud in here, kids." He crossed his arms over his chest. "Loud music. Screaming." He gestured toward the open window. "All of Madison can probably hear you."

Fish cleared his throat. "Sorry, Mr. Reedy, sir. We'll keep it down."

The landlord released a cloud of foul-smelling cigar smoke into the apartment.

Pike swiped at his eyes with his pajama sleeve and backed up toward Dory. She put a hand on his shoulder, eyeing Pop's service flag just inside the door.

"Where's your father?" Reedy leaned against the doorframe. "Hurley, right?"

Dory cringed. She didn't like the way Pop's name sounded in the landlord's mouth.

Fish hesitated. "He's at work."

(Which wasn't a lie. If you want to get technical about it.)

Fulton, evidently relieved that the wailing was over, strolled out of Pop's bedroom.

Reedy cleared what sounded like a very large glob of phlegm from his throat. He looked at the cat. "What the heck is that?"

Dory thought this must be a trick question. "It's a cat."

Reedy scowled. "I can see that. I mean, what's it doing here? No pets allowed."

Fulton made a sharp left and darted behind the sofa, as if he detected a menace.

(He did. Cats are excellent menace detectors.)

"What do you mean?" Dory narrowed her gaze at the landlord. "Mr. Bergen had a cat."

Pike nodded. "His name was Winston. He got run over by a transit bus last summer." Winston had been surly and unpleasant, but they were all sorry anyhow, about the transit bus.

The landlord was entirely unmoved. "Rules change. No pets," he repeated. He licked his lips.

Like Bela Lugosi getting ready to bite someone's neck, Dory thought.

"But, Mr. Reedy," Pike said, his voice small, "he's a stray, you see, so—"

The landlord finished his sentence for him, his voice almost a growl, now. "So he'll be perfectly happy back on the street where you found him."

Dory's heart twisted in her chest. She glanced over her shoulder, where Fulton remained well hidden behind the sofa.

"When will your father be home?" Reedy asked.

Fish cleared his throat. "Later," he said.

Quite a bit later, Dory thought.

"Have him see me." The landlord picked at some dead skin in the corner of his mouth. "And I can explain to him about rules changing." He turned slowly and stepped back into the narrow hallway, then turned again and gestured toward the sofa—toward the cat—with his chin. "Get rid of that animal," he said. "And keep it down."

He slammed the apartment door behind him so hard, it shook the rickety little table by the door. The framed photo of Pop and Mama toppled, hitting the floor with a splintering crack.

They stood there until they heard the landlord close the door to his own apartment. Even Pike seemed to know to keep quiet until Reedy was gone. But at the click of the door to apartment 6 across the hall, he choked out a fresh sob and knelt by the photo. The frame itself was in pieces. Pike picked them up, leaving a storm of glass behind on the floor.

"Watch it, Pike. You'll cut yourself," Fish warned.

Pike sniffled. "I don't care."

Joining his brother on the floor, Fish scooped Pike into his lap.

Dory reached down and extracted the photo from the shards. "The picture's still okay," she whispered.

"It'll be all right," Fish said.

Pike clearly wasn't convinced. He swiped at his nose.

Fish pulled a handkerchief from his pocket and positioned it for his brother. "Blow."

Pike blew.

"We're not getting rid of the cat," Dory said. He had only been hers for a few hours, but she was ready to fight for the creature if Fish disagreed.

He didn't, though. "I know we're not," he whispered, his voice shaky. "The cat we can hide. Producing Pop is another story."

"What are we going to do?" Dory asked.

Fish pocketed the handkerchief but said nothing.

Dory poked him. "Fish?"

Fish ran a hand through his hair. "How should I know, Dor? Pop didn't exactly leave instructions for this."

It was true, Dory supposed. Pop hadn't envisioned a scenario where the old landlord died and the new landlord turned out to be diabolical. Anger boiled in her chest at the very idea of a world in which a villain like Reedy was here in New York while a hero like Pop was "somewhere near Europe."

Fulton emerged from behind the sofa. He wound

himself between the Byrnes, blessing each of them with the caress of his tail.

Fish turned over the busted picture frame. "Let's just clean this up, okay?"

Dory nodded. She went to the hall closet for the broom and the dustpan, and swept up the glass.

As she dumped it into the wastepaper basket in the kitchen, she caught a glimpse of herself in the mirror above the sink. There was still a smudge on her chin from the old hotel.

The old hotel.

Dory ran to the bedroom and pulled the framed photo of Mae from under her bed. It was about the right size. Releasing the catch on the back, she slid out the picture.

"This is okay with you, right, Mae?" she whispered.

Mae smiled back at her.

Dory reversed the photograph, hiding Mae's smile against the backing.

In the living room, Fish was still sitting on the floor, trying to push the pieces of frame back together.

"This should work," Dory said, holding up Mae's frame.

Fish's face was a question mark. "Where'd you get that?"

Dory cleared her throat to give herself a moment to think. "Mrs. Manzetti was going to donate it to a rummage sale at Our Lady of the Rosary, but when I told her it looked too nice for that, she gave it to me."

A rummage sale at Our Lady of the Rosary. For Pete's sake, the lies were just rolling off her tongue now.

The photograph of Pop and Mama fit almost perfectly.

Dory secured the clasp and handed it to Pike, who put it in its place. And the Byrne family—Dory and Fish and Pike in the flesh, Pop and Mama frozen in time on the Coney Island beach—all stood there for a long moment, just looking at one another.

Dory's eyes filled at the sight of her parents' summer-happy smiles. "Be right back," she said. She went to Pop's closet, yanking his favorite shirt from its hanger and wrapping herself up in it. She was already perspiring from the altercation with Reedy, but the worn flannel was soothing. A sort of caress. A sort of armor.

She wanted to write to Pop. Tell him everything. But just now, it felt practically impossible to follow the V-Mail rules and *make it cheerful.*

In the living room, Fish had turned the radio back on, low this time. It was Vaughn Monroe singing "When the Lights Go On Again." They sat on the sofa, Fish in the middle, one arm around Pike, the other around Dory.

"I want Pop to come home," Pike said.

Fish squeezed him closer. "He will."

"He's been gone forever."

"I know it feels that way."

"It *is* that way," Pike said.

"You're right. It is that way," Fish said.

Dory tucked her hands inside the sleeves of Pop's shirt. She knew Fish was only appeasing Pike. Maeve Morrison's father had been gone over a year. Joseph Ricci's even longer. Pop had been gone only six months.

Still. It sure did feel like forever.

SENTINELS
OF
LIBERTY

Teaching a cat to hide turned out to be not all that hard. Tucked into a corner of Pop's closet, a bedside table drawer with a missing knob made an excellent cat box when lined with sand pilfered from a playground sandbox up on Essex. And Fulton never so much as mewed when the Byrnes shut the closet door on him, practicing, in case Reedy knocked again. In fact, he seemed to relish the quiet of the closet, curling himself into a ball on top of one of Pike's old undershirts. If Fulton missed his days as a New York City cat-about-town, you'd never know it.

But, like Fish said, getting rid of Fulton hadn't been Reedy's only demand. He'd also asked to see Pop. And that trick might be harder to pull off. Telling Reedy the truth about Pop was clearly out of the question. If he was the sort of louse who didn't bat an eye at throwing a helpless cat out onto the street, it seemed unlikely that he'd take kindly to the Byrnes' living arrangement. They'd have to try to keep Pop's whereabouts a secret, which meant staying out of Reedy's way as much as possible.

Mrs. Kopek agreed that Reedy was the wrong sort. "I brought him flaki the day he moved in," she said, "and I found it in the bin in the alley when I went to empty my garbage."

She was huffy about it, though Dory remembered Mrs. Kopek making them flaki—tripe soup—a while back, and seemed to recall that it smelled like socks. She couldn't believe she was agreeing with Reedy, but on this point she and the new landlord saw eye to eye.

"Keep your distance," Mrs. Kopek said. "Don't give him any reason to think twice about you. And maybe he'll just forget about your papa."

The Byrnes didn't care for it, having to tiptoe around in their own home, having to look both ways before they used the hallway bathroom. Dory, especially, was grumpy about it, regularly reminding Fish that this was all his fault for telling Pop he could go.

Fish would shake his head. "So you've told me, Dor."

"Well, it's true," Dory would say.

*

What finally ended the grumpiness was Pop's next letter, which came the last Saturday of the month. It included information about where he was: England.

"Well, that's a little more specific, isn't it?" Fish said.

114

But it wasn't the mention of England that resolved Dory's grumpiness. It was the letter's ending that got her:

> *I think what we're doing here matters. Least-*
> *wise, I hope so, because I know it can't be easy*
> *for you three back at home. I'm proud of you,*
> *beloveds, for being so strong.*

Then and there, as Fish read the words out loud, Dory swallowed a lump in her throat and decided the least she could do was prove Pop right.

She shook the funk from her shoulders. "Let's go someplace we don't have to tiptoe. Let's do something fun."

Pike perked up. "Can we go to the movies? I want to see this week's installment of *Captain America*."

"Ugh," Dory grunted. "Boring." It was one of those serialized pictures theaters showed after the newsreel and before the movie you actually wanted to see.

Pike scowled at her. "It's not boring! It's fifteen whole chapters full of *not boring*!"

"Yeah, Dory," Fish said. He folded the letter and put it in the drawer of the side table. "Come on." He nudged Pike. "Get a sweater. Movie theaters are cold."

Pike leaped off the sofa and headed for the bedroom.

Dory elbowed Fish. "You don't want to sit through a whole twenty minutes of *Captain America* any more than I do."

Fish sighed. "Of course I don't."

"So why'd you say we would?"

Fish picked at a frayed spot on the sofa's arm. "Because I want to make Pike happy."

Which was a very simple reason. A very good reason. *It would have been Pop's reason,* Dory thought. She cocked a sideways smile. "Can I pick the movie, at least?"

"Sure."

She got up and checked the listings in Mrs. Kopek's newspaper and grinned at what she found. "Let's go to the Elgin."

Fish groaned. "That's like forty blocks."

"Yep." Dory nodded. "But it'll be worth it. They've got *The Curse of the Cat People.*"

Fish wrinkled his nose. "Not a chance."

Dory returned to the sofa and sank in next to her brother again. "Please?"

"No."

She threw her arms around Fish's middle and wormed her fingers into his rib cage, tickling him until he squirmed with laughter. "Please?" she squealed.

Fish grabbed her wrists and wriggled free. "Fine," he said. "*The Curse of the Cat Monsters.*"

"It's *Cat People.*"

"Whatever."

Dory relaxed against her brother's side. He wasn't Pop, but he was trying, she supposed.

Which is really all a person can do, when it comes down to it.

*

May careened into June the next week, making it awfully difficult to concentrate on school. Through the classroom windows, the students in room 403 could make out summer's laziness approaching through the glass. Miss Ozinskas seemed to understand. Reading assignments grew shorter. Afternoon games of Seven Up grew longer.

Vincent pressed down Dory's thumb every time he was one of the seven. She knew this because she peeked during the thumb-pressing and could see his argyle socks. But when it came time for her to guess who had chosen her, she always picked someone else, afraid her cheeks would get pink if she said Vincent's name out loud.

She supposed this was what happened once you'd danced with a boy.

*

Dory wrote Pop the longest letter she could fit onto V-Mail paper, her handwriting tiny, like it was meant to be read by dolls. *Make it cheerful,* she thought, sitting down to it.

She told him about Fulton. How she'd rescued the cat from a life of squalor. How his ribs had stuck out a lot then, but not so much now that he'd been a Byrne for almost a whole three weeks. How he sat in Pop's chair while they were eating dinner.

She told him about the sixth-grade field trip to the Central Park Zoo. How a boy called Harold Poscowicz (who was the sort of boy who stuck his finger in his mouth and then stuck that same finger into other people's ears) blew wet raspberries at a gorilla named Jocko until Jocko picked up a banana peel and hurled it through the bars of his cage. It was a direct hit, she told Pop. Right to Harold Poscowicz's crummy face.

She shared neighborhood news. How one of the Tsitak twins—Rhea, she thought it was—had started walking. How Mrs. Schmidt had given Fish both crullers *and* pfefernüsse cookies when he passed the bakery yesterday. And how Mrs. Kopek wasn't speaking to the Doyle sisters because they'd used up all the hot water in the hallway bathroom three days in a row.

The list of things Dory didn't tell Pop included the following:

1. The fact that she'd spent the night in an abandoned hotel
2. The fact that Vincent's handkerchief was under her bed
3. The fact that the new landlord was a villain
4. The fact that she missed him so hard, her heart stung

*

The following Monday afternoon, the Byrnes sat on the fire escape in the late-day sun. Fish had bought candy apples from the Pearl Street vendor on his way home from school, and the children were intent on enjoying them.

Pike cut his in pieces and ate it with a fork so he didn't miss a speck. Fish ate his one lick at a time, relishing the sweet pucker of the shell on its own. Dory only got through half of hers before it fell off the stick and plummeted toward Madison Street, smacking the pavement and splattering into the road.

Fish held his out to her. "Want some of mine?"

She wrinkled her nose and shook her head. "It's all licked. But thanks."

Propped on the windowsill, the portable radio played Glenn Miller and his orchestra, "Don't Sit Under the Apple Tree (with Anyone Else but Me)."

Pike stabbed his last chunk. "Can I have a dime, please?"

"What for?" Fish asked.

"To send to Captain America."

Dory picked at a bit of rust on the grate. "What's Captain America need a dime for?"

Pike was wide-eyed at her ignorance. "To muster his army. The Sentinels of Liberty." He paused. "From the back of the comic?"

"What's a sentinel?" Dory asked.

"Like a guardian," Fish said. He nibbled on the last of his apple core. "We haven't got a dime for Captain America right now, Pike. We already splurged on these candy apples."

Pike pouted. "Billy Donnelly's a Sentinel of Liberty."

"Billy Donnelly's a drip." Dory had said it before, but it bore repeating.

Fish reclined on the fire escape grate. Fulton joined him, stepping onto his chest and making himself comfortable.

"But you get an official membership card. And a badge," Pike whined.

Fish took a deep breath, then exhaled slowly, the way Pop did when he was trying to be patient. The cat rose and fell on his chest. "Look, Pike," he said, "we just don't have any extra dimes lying around right now."

Pike pointed through the window at the mayonnaise jar on top of the Frigidaire. "There are loads of dimes in there."

"I know," Fish said. "But they're not for Captain America. At least not right now, okay?"

"Fine." Pike gave an indignant sigh. He got up and lowered himself through the window.

Fish raised himself onto his elbows. "Aw, for Pete's sake, Pike. Don't be sore."

"I'm not sore," Pike said, heading for the door. "I'm just going to the bathroom."

Dory stretched out next to Fish. "He's definitely sore." She felt a pang, thinking how it must be hard, denying a person the chance to become a Sentinel of Liberty.

Fish adjusted the cat and lay back again, defeated. "Yeah."

Dory needed to finish an essay for school tomorrow about Lewis Carroll's "Jabberwocky." Actually, if you want to know the truth, she needed to *start* the essay. All right, the whole truth was, she hadn't even finished reading "Jabberwocky." She'd gotten eight lines in and decided it was ridiculous. "Slithy toves" and "mome raths" and a whole bunch of other nonsense. Honestly. The world was plenty full of nonsense already.

But just now, the slithy toves could wait. The Song

Spinners were singing "Comin' In on a Wing and a Prayer," and the afternoon sun felt glorious on her face. Dory licked a sugar crystal from the corner of her mouth and tapped her foot in time with the music, content.

The song was just ending when the shouting started.

It was coming from the hallway beyond the apartment door but was muted by the burble of the radio, so it took both Dory and Fish a minute to place it.

It wasn't until the radio went silent for a few beats that they realized it was Pike.

Fish was up like a shot, handing the cat to Dory and vaulting through the apartment window. Dory set Fulton on the fire escape and followed, the two of them reaching the apartment door just as Pike threw it open, his face red and panicked.

"The toilet's overflowing!" he shouted. "It's going everywhere!"

In the hallway behind him, water shimmered on the worn wood floor.

Fish leaped into the hall, his feet splatting, and ran for the bathroom. Dory and Pike followed, the water now looking less like a puddle and more like a stream.

Pike was sobbing.

Which didn't stop Dory from interrogating him. "What did you do, Pike?" she shouted.

Fish threw open the bathroom door, letting out a rush of water.

Tears streamed down Pike's face. "I tried to make it stop, but I didn't know how!"

Dory watched, breathless, as Fish slipped on the flooded tiles, catching himself on the sink. Water continued to pour over the toilet's rim, out the bathroom door, and down the fourth-floor hallway, heading for the stairs.

Fish made it to the toilet and crouched, reaching for the valve at the back of the tank. The shutoff knob made a shrieking sound as he wrenched it to the off position. The dastardly hiss of the toilet tank slowed, then stopped. And with it the flooding.

He stood and wiped his hands on his pants.

Dory looked at Pike, exasperated. "That's how you make it stop."

Pike choked out a sob. "I'm sorry!"

Fish opened his arms and let his brother run to him, picking Pike up and enfolding him. "It's all right," Fish murmured, still breathing hard after all the panic.

But the panic, as it turned out, was only just beginning.

Reedy appeared from his apartment, the sneer that seemed to be a permanent fixture on his face becoming nothing short of grotesque as he took in the mess.

The Byrnes froze, Pike squeezing his eyes shut against Fish's shoulder.

The landlord's voice held no sympathy. "That's it," he snarled. "That's it." He looked at the three of them, his eyes so dark, Dory's blood ran cold.

"Get your father," Reedy said. The words came out strangled. "Right now."

Fish shifted Pike to his hip so he could put an arm

around Dory. She welcomed the embrace, though she could feel her brother trembling.

"We'll get this cleaned up, Mr. Reedy," Fish said. The tremble was in his throat, too.

Reedy's upper lip was beaded with sweat. "I'm not leaving that to a pack of hooligan kids," he said. "I'm done dealing with you three. I want to talk to your father."

"He's not home," Fish said.

"You've got to be kidding me," Reedy barked. He splashed down the hall toward the Byrnes' still-open door and barged right in, Dory and Fish following with mouths agape at the intrusion, Pike whimpering on Fish's shoulder.

"What the heck is going on?" the landlord shouted as he stomped through the Byrnes' apartment on a rampage. "I've been here more than a month now, and I've never even seen the guy." His eyes darted from one to the other of them.

And then to Fulton. Who had chosen an inopportune moment to come in from the fire escape. The cat felt the fizz of the landlord's rage and darted down the hall for Pop's room.

Reedy's voice became a hiss. "What did I tell you about pets?"

Fish cleared his throat. "That they're not allowed, sir. But we were just trying to—"

"I don't care what you were trying to do," Reedy wheezed. "I'm done dealing with you lousy kids," he repeated, throwing his hands in the air and turning for the door. "If your father hasn't shown up and explained how he's going to keep you three in line by the time I—"

The Byrnes watched in horror as the landlord's eyes lit on Pop's flag.

Blue star. White background. Red border. Gold fringe. There, above the rickety table.

Reedy faced the children again.

The air in the apartment turned rancid. Dory felt like she couldn't draw a breath. She glanced at Fish. He glanced back at her.

She thought quick. "That's our uncle's service flag," she whispered.

The landlord gave a mirthless chuckle. "Sure it is."

"Dory's right." Fish's voice was pleading. "That's our uncle's."

Reedy took a deep breath.

For a fleeting moment, Dory thought perhaps the blue star would soften him.

It didn't.

"I don't know what you're trying to pull here," he said. "But this isn't an orphanage."

Fish tightened his grip on Pike and Dory.

"If there's no guardian here..." Reedy looked at Fish. "No *adult* guardian," he added. "No adult guardian *who signed the lease*, then it's the city that'll have to deal with you." He shook his head again. "I don't know what kind of father leaves his kids to become delinquents, but it's not my job to babysit you."

Rage bubbled in Dory's chest. Calling them delinquents was one thing, but talking bad about Pop was a bridge too far. She wanted to claw Reedy's eyes out. Kick him in the shins just as hard as she could. Grab him by his filthy T-shirt and toss him off the fire escape. She gritted her teeth and heaved deep breaths. Dug her fingernails into Fish's side.

"Listen, Mr. Reedy," Fish said. "Let's just—"

"I'm done listening," Reedy snarled. "I'm reporting you to the city."

He turned with a grunt and left the apartment, slamming the door behind him.

The radio, still murmuring by the window, played the Andrews Sisters. It was a song about somebody's papa leaving for the war. The Byrnes were all too stunned to notice the irony. They stood there for a long moment, their hearts in their throats at Reedy's threat.

It was Dory who moved first, going to the door and slipping the deadbolt. Just now, she wished they had more than one, the landlord's breach so raw and terrifying. She held her ear to the doorframe and listened for him. He'd be back in the hall with a mop and towels any minute now, she guessed, to clean up the mess.

She turned to her brothers. "Let's go back outside where he can't hear us."

Fish nodded. He boosted Pike through the window, let Dory follow, and brought up the rear. The three of them bunched together against the side railing, Fish in the middle, Pike and Dory on either side.

Dory looked up at him. "What are we going to do?"

Fish raised his eyes toward the sky, thinking or praying or both. "I don't know."

"He said he's going to report us to the city."

"I heard, Dor."

"Are they going to put us in the foundling home?" Pike cried.

Dory shook her head. "Nobody's putting me in the foundling home."

"Nobody's putting anybody anywhere," Fish whispered. He kissed the top of Pike's head.

Dory chewed on her thumbnail. "We'll just never answer the apartment door again. That way, the city can't find us."

Fish sighed. "The city can always find us. And besides, Dor, that's no way to live."

She spit out a piece of thumbnail. "What do they do when they find you?" she asked. "Do they come with nets or something?" She was picturing the operation working something like the dogcatchers she saw on Broadway sometimes.

Fish shook his head. "I don't think they come with nets." But he didn't sound confident.

Pike gave a shudder, his crying jag burning itself out. "I'm sorry I flooded the bathroom."

Dory cleared her throat. "Not just the bathroom."

"Dor," Fish warned.

"I'm just saying." Dory shrugged. "It was the hall, too."

Fish kissed Pike's head again. "It was an accident."

Pike hugged his knees. "I'm scared."

"I know, Pike."

"Maybe we should ask Mrs. Kopek if we can live with her," Pike said.

Fish winced.

"What good would that do?" Dory asked. "We'd still be here in the building for Reedy and the city to find us."

"What about the Morellos? They're down the street," Pike offered.

Dory's heart lurched. Move in with Vincent? "Their apartment's tiny," she said. "Just like everyone else we know."

Pike was insistent. "There's got to be somebody we could ask. Pop always says that the neighborhood will give us what we need."

Fish heaved a sigh. "He meant Mrs. Kopek sharing her newspaper and Mrs. Morello checking up on us when we pass each other on Madison, Pike. He didn't mean sleeping on their living room floors. He didn't mean mooching."

Like pickles and desserts, mooching was apparently against Fish's rules.

"What are we going to do, then?" Dory asked again.

Fish massaged his eyes with his fingertips. "I'll think of something."

It wasn't the first time he'd said that. It also wasn't the first time a plan had not been forthcoming. Coming up with plans was not something Fish was especially good at.

Dory settled back against the fire escape and let her brother put his arm around her shoulders. Putting his arm around her shoulders was something he *was* especially good at.

She'd figure out a plan herself.

Below them, someone coughed. Dory looked down, glimpsing Mr. Kowalczyk at his window. He withdrew when their eyes met.

Her cheeks flamed. He'd been listening to every single tearfully embarrassing second of their conversation. Even in midair, forty or fifty feet above the street, the city offered no privacy. She stuck her tongue out at his open window.

She set her jaw. Wriggled from under Fish's arm and stood, retreating through the window and returning a moment later, her palm outstretched toward Pike. In it was the dime she'd retrieved from the cash register in the old hotel.

"For Captain America," she said.

She looked at Fish's raised eyebrows.

"It didn't come from the mayonnaise jar. It's my own money. I...I found it."

His face solemn, Pike took the dime. "Thanks."

"Sure," Dory said.

The way she figured, they could use a Sentinel of Liberty in the family right about now.

BLINK. BLINK. BLINK. **BEAM.**

The next day was the sixth of June.

School would be out for the summer on Friday, and at PS 42, the students in room 403 had begun the morning by cleaning the classroom in preparation for the end of the year. Everyone's desks and chairs had to have the chewing gum scraped off the bottoms of them so that next year's sixth grade would have a fresh start. Chewing gum wasn't officially allowed, of course, but it made its way in anyhow. Neither Dory nor Rosemary cared for the stuff, so while Gerald Levinski (who was partial to Wrigley's Doublemint) spent a half an hour hunched over his upturned chair regretting the errors of his youth, they were free to sit at their desks and talk.

It was largely Rosemary talking. About her summer plans. She was going to spend most of it at her nonna's in Hackensack. "To escape the heat," she explained. As far as Dory knew, Hackensack was only fifteen or twenty miles away. She wasn't sure how much effect that kind of a distance would have on climate. But having a nonna sure sounded nice. And any sort of escape—Hackensack or otherwise—was appealing to Dory at the moment.

"How big's your grandmother's apartment?" she asked.

"One bedroom." Rosemary shrugged. "I'll sleep on the sofa. But it's only a block from the movie theater, so Nonna says we can go to the pictures anytime. Doesn't that sound divine?"

"Yeah." Dory nodded. "Divine."

But not divine enough to accommodate three more.

At around a quarter to nine, as Gerald deposited the last of his calcified gum into the wastepaper basket, the door to room 403 opened with a thwack and a pink-faced boy stumbled in with a twitchy grin on his face.

"Miss Ozinskas! Miss Ozinskas! We've stormed the beaches at Normandy!"

The teacher went pale. "We've done what? Slow down, Jamie."

"Where's Normandy?" Evie Sullivan asked, without raising her hand.

"The north coast of France," Miss Ozinskas said. "Just across the channel from England."

Dory blinked at the mention of England. That's where Pop was.

Miss Ozinskas turned her attention back to Jamie. "Now. Slowly and carefully, please. Tell us what's happened."

Jamie's cheeks were flushed. "Us and the Tommies—I

mean the English." He was breathless. "General Eisen-hower said. Even the Krauts are reporting it."

Miss Ozinskas corrected him. "The Germans."

"Right. The Germans. Even they're reporting it. We're wiping them out! We're winning! Principal Morgan sent me to tell you."

"Is that all the information you have for us?"

Jamie nodded.

"Well, thank you very much indeed."

Jamie took off at a sprint as Miss Ozinskas's class erupted into cheering and clapping.

Dory chewed on her thumbnail, exchanging glances with the other students whose pops were away: Maeve, John, Joseph, Vincent, Evie, Ernest, Corrinne, Ronald. She didn't know exactly where their fathers were—though she seemed to recall that John's and Joseph's and Corrinne's were in the Pacific. Which she thought was maybe not anywhere near France.

She wondered if Pop was storming a beach at Normandy.

She wondered if storming a beach was dangerous.

She wondered if Reedy had ratted them out to the city yet.

It was an awful lot to wonder about.

* * *

She and Pike met Fish at the public library after school. Just in case Reedy *had* ratted them out, they figured it was best to stay away from the apartment until later, when the foundling-catchers from the city were less likely to be out with their nets.

The library part was Pike's idea.

They found a table by the window in the children's reading room and settled in.

"Normandy's in France," Pike said. "That's what Mrs. Denton told us."

"Miss Ozinskas told us that too," Dory said.

"But Pop's in England, right?"

There was a furrow between Fish's eyebrows. "He was."

"Is he in France now?"

Fish ran a hand through his hair. "I don't know."

"What does *storming a beach* mean?" Pike asked.

Fish bent his head this way and that. Dory heard his neck crack.

"It means invading." He looked like Pike's questions were making his brain itch.

"But why are we invading France?" Pike continued. "And not Germany?"

Fish cleared his throat. "Because the Nazis have control of France. We're taking it back."

"Oh." Pike considered this. "Everybody seems to think that storming beaches is pretty swell."

"Yeah," Dory agreed. "But not everybody has a pop off fighting."

"Is Pop okay, do you think?" Pike asked.

"Sure, Pike," Fish said. "Pop's fine."

It was the right answer, Dory thought. *The only answer*

any of them wanted. She looked at Fish, the furrow in his brow more of a canyon now, and nodded.

"I'll bet Pop's killed loads of Krauts already," Pike said.

"Germans," Fish corrected.

"Billy Donnelly calls them Krauts."

"Billy Donnelly's a drip," Dory reminded him.

From across the reading room, she spotted Vincent and his sister in the doorway. She sat up a little straighter.

On the other side of the table, Fish did the same. He raised a hand in greeting, and Dory watched his forehead go smooth and his eyes light up the way any seventeen-year-old boy's might. It had been a while, she realized, since Fish looked seventeen.

There were greetings all around. Irene said she and Vincent were there to return some books their mother had borrowed. Then she and Fish struck up a conversation about a geometry test, and Pike announced that he was going to look at books, leaving Dory and Vincent paired off on the other side of the table.

"Any word from your pop?" Vincent asked.

Dory nodded. "Last week. He said he was in England. Which I guess means maybe he was part of that beach storming?"

"Mine too," Vincent said.

"Oh." Dory paused. "I suppose it's better, knowing where they are at least."

"Yeah. I s'pose." Vincent swallowed hard. "I'm scared, though."

133

It was startling, Vincent's admission. But also comforting somehow.

"Me too," Dory said.

"Jeez, Dory." Vincent gave a wry grin. "I didn't think you were scared of anything."

Dory looked at her feet. "I guess I just ruined my reputation, then."

"I guess." Vincent chuckled. "So what are you doing here? All three of you?"

"We're hiding from our landlord," Dory said.

Vincent's eyes went wide. "Really?"

"Uh-huh."

"I guess things haven't gotten better since you dumped soup on him?" Vincent wrinkled his nose.

Dory shook her head. "Not by a long shot."

She proceeded to tell Vincent every detail of the mess with Reedy.

He shook his head in disbelief. "I was wondering why you hadn't hung your pop's flag back up." He paused. "But your landlord wouldn't really rat you out to the city, would he?"

"I think he would."

"Well, then... what are you going to do?"

Dory shrugged. "We'll figure something out." She sounded more confident than she felt, not having anything in the way of a plan.

She and Vincent sat in silence for a long while.

It wasn't awkward. Not even a little.

Dory's neck didn't itch. Not even a little.

"You know what, Dory?" Vincent said at last. "If you want to, you could hang your pop's flag in our window."

Dory's mouth fell open.

"I'm sure my ma wouldn't mind. And that way, you'd still be able to see it when you pass." Vincent cleared his throat. "And the rest of the world could, too."

It was the kindest thing anybody had ever offered her.

Maybe the kindest thing anybody had ever offered anybody.

"Oh, jeez, Vincent, I..." She felt her nose go all drippy at the startling benevolence. "It's hung just inside the..." She sniffled. "We're okay, but..." Sniffled again. "Thanks."

Vincent produced a neatly pressed handkerchief from his trouser pocket.

Dory blew her nose. Looked at him with a tiny smile. Held up the sodden handkerchief for a moment before stuffing it into her sleeve.

"I'm starting a collection," she said.

*

They stayed until the library closed, long after Vincent and Irene had said their goodbyes.

"Let's not go home quite yet," Fish said, out on East Broadway. "Just in case. Let's just knock around for a while." He raised his eyebrows. "Till it's closer to dark."

It was terrible, fearing home. But Dory and Pike nodded in grim understanding.

New York, however, was anything but grim.

Wherever they ambled, the city was all jubilation.

Mrs. Schmidt called to them from the steps of the bakery and gave them a bag of crullers. "Victory crullers," she said, when she handed the sack to Fish. She called Pike a lamb and pinched his cheeks. She told Dory to comb her hair.

A sign outside the synagogue on Cherry Street announced that it would be open all night for special services. ALL ARE WELCOME, it read. Outside St. Teresa's, the sign said INVASION DAY—COME IN AND PRAY FOR ALLIED VICTORY.

Mr. Aaronson waved to them from the delicatessen. "It's about time we had some happy news, eh, Byrnes?" He gave them each a slice of salami. None of them knew what salami had to do with beaches being stormed in France, but they said thank you all the same.

Outside a Red Cross blood donation center, two sailors danced a jig, the tails of their neckerchiefs flapping every which way.

Beaming smiles and hopeful faces met the Byrnes everywhere they turned.

They walked until the sun began to sink on the historic day, then stopped for groceries at the corner market on Henry Street. Outside, a small crowd gathered around a man with a portable radio broadcasting the news. "The eyes of the world are upon you," a voice said.

"Is that General Eisenhower talking?" Fish asked.

A man in a fedora answered him. "Yep."

"The tide has turned! The free men of the world are marching together to Victory!" the general said. "I have full confidence in your courage, devotion to duty and skill in battle. We will accept nothing less than full Victory!"

The man grinned. "Full victory sounds pretty good, huh, kids?"

Dory, Fish, and Pike all nodded.

"You got a brother or something over there?" the man asked.

"Our pop," Fish said.

"I could see it on your faces." The man winked. "It'll be full victory. Don't you worry."

The Byrnes smiled at the kindness.

"What?" the man said. "Don't you believe me? Can't you feel it?" He held up a hand, indicating Manhattan at large. "Whole city's celebrating." He gestured south. "Even Lady Liberty's lit up about it."

Dory's eyes went wide. "Huh?"

"The statue," the man said. "It's blinking. Giving us a little light show to celebrate."

Dory's heart jumped. "But she's—I mean, *it's*—it's been dark for years."

The man's eyes sparkled. "Not tonight."

For a moment, Dory couldn't hear the voice on the radio or the murmur of the crowd or the cars passing on Henry Street. Only the news about Libby.

"Thanks, mister," she said, then turned to Fish and grabbed his sleeve. "I have to go see."

"What?" Fish said. "What are you talking about, Dory? It's nearly dark."

"I have to go see," she repeated.

137

"But it's time for dinner. We just bought groceries."

"It's way past time for dinner," Pike said. "And I'm hungry."

"Besides," Fish said, "we're supposed to stick together, right?"

Dory's chest felt all fizzy. Libby was trying to tell her something. If she waited, she might miss it. "Please, Fish," she said. "Please."

Fish looked at her. He must have seen the desperation in her eyes.

"Go fast," he said. "And be careful."

"I'm hungry," Pike said again.

"Start dinner," Dory shouted, already running. "Just save me some!"

✳

She didn't slow down for at least ten blocks. As she crossed under the elevated train line just below Pearl, she got a stitch in her side and had to stop and breathe for a second.

A lady in a flowered dress stooped to check on her. "Are you all right, dear?"

"Fine, thanks," Dory said. She took off again, past the turn for the ferry terminal, through the scrubby grass of Battery Park, and over the rubble that surrounded the Castle. A crowd had gathered. Big for this hour, when Battery Park was usually vacant. Big enough to block her view. She nudged people aside to get to her usual climbing spot and made it to the top of the ramparts. A man below shouted at her to be careful as she scrambled over the edge and rose to her feet, turning at last to face the harbor.

And there she was.

Libby was a spectacle.

She'd been shrouded in darkness for so many nights, the sight of it was startling. Her torch burned like an actual flame. And the patterned pulse of the lights in her crown was mesmerizing. *Blink. Blink. Blink.* The first three short. *Beam.* The last one long.

Dory stood there alone above the crowd. Breathless.

Again, the three short flashes, followed by the single long pulse of brilliance.

It wasn't just a light show. Dory knew it in her bones. It was some kind of message.

Blink. Blink. Blink. Beam.

"What are you trying to tell me, Libby?" she whispered.

She didn't have Pop's binoculars, of course, but Dory's eyes knew every inch of the statue's toes, her gown, the book she held in her left hand.

Blink. Blink. Blink. Beam.

She looked at the statue's right arm. The one holding the torch.

There were stairs in there, Dory knew. People used to be able to walk all the way up through the goddess's shoulder, elbow, wrist. All the way into the torch itself. Then, back during the Great War, the Germans had bombed the munitions depot at Black Tom Island, only a couple thousand feet away, wounding Libby's arm so badly that nobody'd been in it since.

Blink. Blink. Blink. Beam.

Nobody'd been in there in years.

Blink. Blink. Blink. Beam.

In decades.

Blink. Blink. Blink. Beam.

Dory's heart swelled.

Blink. Blink. Blink. Beam.

A smile spread across her face.

Blink. Blink. Blink. Beam.

She knew another place nobody'd been in for a long, long time.

(Well. Almost nobody.)

Dory offered Libby a slow nod of understanding. Of gratitude. The Green Goddess was looking out for her, all right. What more evidence could you want?

Making her way down the wall and over the rubble, Dory headed north along the riverfront, her heart plunking the same pattern as Libby's message.

Blink. Blink. Blink. Beam.

✳

Caputo's was closed when she passed.

Turning left on Beekman, Dory paused at the back alley. She looked up at the boarded windows of the third, fourth, and fifth floors, the looming mass of the old hotel, and gave a bark of a laugh. It echoed off the alley walls.

She skipped toward home.

Skipping was not something Dory Byrne was prone to doing.

But this was a special occasion.

A historic one, even. For both Dory and the world at large. Though the world at large was the last thing on Dory's mind just now. All she could think about was the message Libby had handed her, plain as day.

At the corner of Catherine and Madison, she looked both ways to make sure Reedy was nowhere in sight. Her feet pounded up the fire escape stairs, pausing only on the third-floor landing, where Mr. Kowalczyk sat at his window.

"It's gonna be okay, Mr. Kowalczyk!" she shouted.

She didn't wait for a reply, climbing the final set of stairs and hurling herself through the already-open window.

Pike and Fish, intent on the radio, startled at her entrance.

"Shh," Fish said. "The president's praying."

"Okay, but—" Dory started.

"Shh," Fish said again. "Respect, Dory."

". . . a peace that will let all of men live in freedom, reaping the just rewards of their honest toil," the president said. "Thy will be done, Almighty God. Amen."

Pike and Fish looked up at Dory.

Wiping sweat from her brow, she grinned from ear to ear.

"I've got a plan."

MOSTLY ABOUT
THE
GLOATING

Despite their pleas, Dory didn't tell Pike and Fish the specifics. While she had every confidence that her plan was a good one—a perfect one, even—she knew Fish wouldn't agree to it if he heard about it in advance. If she told him, Fish would:

1. Realize she'd lied to him
2. Panic
3. Squash the plan

This would all happen anyway, she supposed, but Dory thought it best that it happen while they were standing in front of the dumbwaiter with no other choice as to where to go.

All she told them was to pack the necessities—some clothes, some food, some V-Mail paper, the portable radio, the mayonnaise jar from on top of the Frigidaire—by Friday night.

"School'll be out." Dory grinned. "So it's a perfect time for a vacation."

Fish's eyes goggled. "We can't afford a vacation."

"It's not gonna cost us anything," she clarified.

He squinted at her. "And I told you, we're not mooching off the neighborh—"

"No mooching, Fish. I know."

"Dory, what are we—"

"Friday night," Dory said. "Just be ready."

✳

She managed the preparations after school the next day, while Fish took Pike to hide out at the library.

Zukowski's Hardware on East Broadway was more than just a hardware store. It had hardware, sure, but also an odd collection of junk, old and new. The Byrnes had always liked going there with Pop when he needed to pick up lightbulbs or twine or some other grown-up thing. Pop's first job, when he was fourteen, was stocking the shelves at Zukowski's, and even all these years later, Mr. Zuk still welcomed him back with a gap-toothed grin and that hug that old men do—a sloppy, one-armed affair with a lot of back-slapping.

"Hurley's baby girl!" Mr. Zuk shouted. He greeted Dory with the "got your nose" trick.

Pike still fell for that sort of thing, but Dory was too old. Besides which, she had always preferred the one where the person reaches behind your ear and extracts the nickel or butterscotch candy that you didn't know was stashed back there. But when Mr. Zuk held up his hand, his thumb protruding between his index and middle fingers, she smiled.

"What's the news from your papa?" he asked. "When did you last hear from him?"

"A couple weeks ago. He was in England. So we think he was part of the invasions."

"Your papa's strong. He'll be okay." Mr. Zuk pressed his lips together. "You here to visit, or you need something?"

Dory cleared her throat to make way for the lies. "Me and Fish and Pike are going camping."

"Camping!" Mr. Zuk's head backed up on his neck. "You mean, the sleeping-outside kind of camping? You're city kids! Where are you gonna find someplace to sleep outside?"

Dory hadn't yet developed the lie in this much detail. She thought fast and named the first place that came to mind. "Staten Island."

Mr. Zuk blinked at her. "Staten Island?"

Maybe people didn't go camping in Staten Island. "Um...yes?"

"You got a tent?"

She nodded. "Pike got one for Christmas." (Also a lie. What Pike had actually gotten for Christmas was a magnifying glass, a book called *Homer Price*, and a can of condensed milk, the latter of which he ate with a spoon until he made himself sick. But the tent story was a nice touch.)

"Okay. So what else do you need?"

Dory consulted her mental list. "Matches, flashlight batteries, and candles."

Mr. Zuk ferreted under the counter and emerged with a box of flashlight batteries. "Here you go," he said. "And matches..." He looked at her. "A lighter'll work better, you know." He dragged a stepstool to the end of the counter and reached for a high shelf. "They're not making these for anybody but soldiers right now. I've got some left over from before, though. You ought to have one, just like your papa." Mr. Zuk climbed down and set a Zippo lighter on the counter.

Dory beamed. "Thanks, Mr. Zuk."

"No problem. Now, candles?" He pointed at the gardening supplies. "Back corner. Go left at the end of that aisle. What kind you want?"

The kind that fit in a sconce in a secret hotel nobody's been in for fifty years, Dory thought. "Just regular candles."

She found what she guessed were the right size and grabbed a bunch, never considering that a dozen or more candles was an awful lot for an overnight camping trip. But Mr. Zuk didn't even blink when she brought them to the counter. He only added them to the pile. Then held up a finger and disappeared into the back room for a minute, returning with a battered kerosene lamp. "Take this, too," he said. "In case Pike gets scared out there in the wilderness of Staten Island."

Dory fingered the dollar she'd gotten out of the mayonnaise jar. "Gee, thanks, Mr. Zuk, but I didn't bring enough money for that."

He waved a hand like he was shooing a fly. "Pah! Byrne money's no good here. Send your brothers my best."

"Aw, jeez, Mr. Zuk. You don't have to—"

"Pah!" He waved his hand again. "It'll be like I'm camping with you." He paused. "Except that you wouldn't catch me sleeping outside if my life depended on it."

Dory grinned at him. "Thanks again, Mr. Zuk."

✳

The moon shone through rain clouds coming in from the east as they climbed down the fire escape late Friday night.

Fish carried a sack of clothes in one hand, a sack of food in the other.

Dory carried her schoolbag, packed with supplies.

Pike carried the cat.

"Come on, Dory. Now you've gotta tell us," Fish said. "Where are we going?"

Dory pointed toward the water. "That way."

Fish rolled his eyes. "That's not what I—"

"Just walk."

By the time they turned on Beekman, a fine mist had gathered, leaving tiny beads on their eyelashes.

"Dory, it's going to rain," Fish said. "Where—"

She nudged them into the alley behind Caputo's. "Here."

"Here?" Fish squinted at her, shielding his eyes from the mist, which was now maybe more of a mizzle. "What do you mean, *here*? Caputo's is closed now. And besides, we're—" He broke off and looked up at the back wall of

the building. Even in the dim light, Dory could see reali-
zation pass over his face like the storm clouds gathering
on the river.

He shook his head. "No way."

"What?" Pike asked. "What's no way?"

Dory kept her eyes on Fish. "I knew you'd say that."

"Of course I'd say that!" he hissed. "You can't be serious, Dory!"

Dory threw her arm over her head to act as a hood.
"Have you got a better idea?"

Fish wrinkled his nose in a scowl. "No, but I—you
just—we can't—" The mizzle now became plain old rain.
He set down the bags and held the side of his jacket out.
"Get under here, Pike, before you get soaked and catch a
cold."

Dory hoisted herself onto the trash bin and opened
Caputo's kitchen window with a grating squeak.

"No," Fish said.

Fulton made a sort of bleating noise.

Her feet balanced on either side of the trash, Dory
turned and looked at the sodden animal. "Pass me the
cat, please."

"Get down," Fish said.

Dory heaved a sigh and slid herself through the
kitchen window as thunder rumbled in the distance. Fulton startled at the sound, leaping from Pike's arms to the
top of the trash bin, then into Dory's waiting hands. She
released him into Caputo's kitchen.

(Which was very likely a serious health code violation.)

Fish wrapped his jacket tighter around Pike. "I mean it, Dor. This is ridiculous. Get back down here."

"I'm wet and cold," Pike whined.

Dory smirked. "It's warm as toast in here."

The thunder clapped again, closer this time, and the patter of raindrops grew louder. Fish swiped a hand through his hair, which was now sending a small rivulet of rain into his eyes. He glowered at Dory, shook his head, and lifted Pike onto his shoulders so he could reach the windowsill. Dory hauled him in the rest of the way, then extended a hand to help Fish.

"No, thank you," Fish grunted. He pushed himself onto the rim of the trash bin and reached for the sill. His right foot slipped, coming down with a slurp in a puddle of fish guts.

Dory extended her hand again. Partly to be helpful, and partly to gloat.

(It was mostly about the gloating. If we're being honest here.)

This time, Fish took her hand and jumped, sliding through Caputo's kitchen window on his stomach and landing in a dripping heap on the drainboard.

He was panting. "I swear, Dory, you just wait until Pop gets home, and—"

"Oh!" Pike exclaimed, getting it at last. "Are we going to try out that dumbwaiter?"

Dory waggled her eyebrows at him and nodded. She spotted Fulton, who was sitting on a stack of clean plates—well, dirty plates now—and scooped him up.

"No," Fish said, brushing the rain from his jacket and shaking a glob of fish guts off his shoe, then picking it up and tossing it into the sink in disgust. "We're not getting in any such thing, Pike."

Dory opened her bag and nestled Fulton on top of the candles. "Yes we are." She extended a hand, which Pike took gladly. "Let's go."

She and Pike left the kitchen and headed for the stairs. Fish followed, grunting in protest.

In the second-floor storage room, Pike looked in wonder at more canned goods than he'd ever thought possible. Dory put down her bag, cat and all, and began shifting Coca-Cola crates.

"What are you doing?" Fish hissed.

She set down the first crate, then tapped the door. "The dumbwaiter's in here," she said. "We've gotta move these, just enough to get the door open. It'll go faster if you help."

Fish's attention shifted briefly to Pike, who was inspecting the toilet brush. "Don't touch that, Pike. It's filthy." He turned back to Dory and took her gently by the arm. "Look, I'm sorry, Dor." He was trying a softer approach, it seemed. "Really. I'm sorry I yelled at you out there." He ran a hand through his wet mop of hair. "I'm the one who said no mooching, and I didn't come up with a plan, and you...you did, and...Thank you."

"You're welcome." Dory wriggled from his grasp and moved the second crate.

Fish shook his head. "But let's just stop, okay? Let's

stay here until the rain ends, and then we'll head home for the night."

Dory hoisted the third crate and added it to the pile. "You said it yourself, Fish. We can't mooch, and jumping out of our skins every time there's a noise in the hallway is no way to live. You start at the Navy Yard next week, and I'm not spending the whole summer in the library with Pike."

From behind the celery salt, Pike grunted.

Fish looked at the dumbwaiter door, panic in his eyes. "Dory, you can't be serious about getting in that thing. There's no way it'll hold us."

She smiled gently. "It will."

"You heard what Mr. Caputo said. The ropes are probably all rotted away. Nobody's been in it for fifty years."

Dory took a deep breath. "Somebody has."

The furrow in Fish's brow became a chasm. "Who? Who's been in it?"

Picking up the fourth crate of Coca-Cola, she gave him a sheepish smile.

Fish's mouth hung open. "No."

Dory kept on smiling.

"When?" Fish whispered. "How?"

"Remember when I asked if I could sleep over at Rosemary's after the dance?"

Fish closed his eyes and threw his head back in defeat.

Pike's voice came from behind a shelf. "Oyster crackers! Can I have some?"

"No," Dory and Fish replied at once.

Dory looked long and hard at her brother. "I'm sorry I lied to you, Fish."

"Yeah. Right."

"No, really." She tucked her damp hair behind her ears. "I only lied because I knew you'd never let me if I told you what I was really doing."

"That's for sure." Fish glanced at the ceiling. "What's up there?" he whispered.

Pike came out from behind a sack of flour. "Treasure?"

Dory shook her head. Though she wasn't actually so sure anymore. It's funny how a person's definition of treasure can change. "It's an old hotel."

She twisted the latch with a flourish, revealing the gaping dumbwaiter.

Fish let out a long, low whistle. He leaned inside and looked up at the pitch-black shaft above. "I can't believe you got in this thing, Dor."

Dory shrugged. "I didn't just get in it, you know. I tested it out with potatoes first."

"Huh." Fish cocked his head at her. "Good thinking."

She stepped into the iron cage. "I think it'll hold all three of us."

Fish crossed his arms and stepped back. "You *think*?"

"Just get in," Dory said. Of course, when she'd potato-tested the contraption, she hadn't anticipated holding a party in there, but she recalled it feeling solid enough. "If it groans too much, we'll..." Well, if it groaned too much, she didn't know what they'd do. The dumbwaiter being the only way up and all. "Just get in," she said again, pressing her back to the cage wall to make room for her brothers.

Pike obeyed without hesitation. From above, the winch gave a whine of complaint at the addition of his forty-five pounds. He wove his fingers together under his chin. "Come on, Fish!"

Fish wiped sweat from his upper lip.

"If you want," Dory said, "I can take Pike up and then come back for you."

Pike's face fell. "No way. I'm not staying up there by myself in the dark."

"Right." Dory excused herself around the cat, pulled out the flashlight, flipped the switch, and handed it to Pike. "You can hold this."

Pike shined the beam up the shaft. "Do you think there are rats up there?"

Dory nodded. "Definitely."

From inside her bag, Fulton grunted his approval.

Fish shook his head. "I can't believe I'm doing this." He took a tentative step into the dumbwaiter. From high above, the pulley shrieked in protest, but the car only dropped an inch or so. He looked at Dory, his face white with terror in the flashlight's patchy glow. "Now what?"

Dory closed and latched the dumbwaiter door. "We pull." She grabbed the rope on the left and handed it to Fish, keeping hold of the lower part of it herself and shifting her position to give them both room to heave in the cramped cage.

Fish gave a trembling nod. "On three?" He looked up at the shaft.

"Yep. On three. But don't look up," Dory said. "It's dusty, and you'll get a snootful."

"Okay." Fish lowered his head. "One."

Dory nodded. "Two."

Fish squeezed his eyes shut. "Three."

As one, he and Dory heaved, sending the dumbwaiter eight or ten inches into the shaft.

"Wheeeeeeee!" Pike squealed as a storm of dust descended from above.

"Again," Dory said.

They hung on the rope, raising themselves another turn of the pulley.

"And again," she said.

Ten more inches.

Fish looked up as the ancient contraption released another shower of dust and grime. He shook his head and blinked furiously.

Pike shrugged. "She told you not to look up."

Fish swiped at his eyes with the heel of his hand. "Keep pulling."

Six more good pulls, and they were at the third floor.

Dory let go of the rope, stretched her fingers, and tipped an imaginary hat at her brothers.

"Welcome to the South Street Hotel."

She swept an arm toward the lobby and bowed deeply. "Enjoy your stay."

PEOPLE MOSTLY
LOOK
DOWN

The boys stepped off the dumbwaiter as if in a dream.
Fish gave another low whistle, taking in the faded
wallpaper, the cracked ceiling, the reception desk. He turned
a full circle, gaping.

Dory stepped forward, threw her arms around her
brother, and hugged him. This surprised everyone, includ-
ing Dory. "You did it, Fish," she said. She could feel him
trembling.

He planted a distracted kiss on the top of her head
and released her. "Jeez Louise, this is nuts," he whispered.

Pike swung the flashlight's beam from side to side
until it landed on the door to room 3. He gave a yelp and
leaped backward onto Dory's foot, then grabbed her by
her shirtsleeve. "Something's watching us."

Dory took the flashlight and illuminated room 3's doorframe. "Don't be a scaredy-cat, Pike. It's just a glass eye."

Fish inhaled sharply. "Sure." He nodded. "Just a glass eye. Nothing creepy about that." From outside, they could hear thunder. "And that doesn't make it creepier at all," he added.

"Bathroom's over there." Dory pointed. "It works, but the water's a little brown. Probably better to use the sinks in Caputo's for drinking." She gestured back toward the dumbwaiter. "We'll probably want to sleep in the biggest room, which is on the top floor," she said. "It's all a little dirty, so if we're going to get any sleep tonight, we should probably start by cleaning that room up."

"A little dirty," Fish echoed.

They made their way back into the dumbwaiter and hauled themselves to the top, where Pike and Fish gawked at the billiard table, still uncovered from Dory's visit.

"Holy moly!" Pike exclaimed. "Can we play?"

Dory shone the light on the rack of cue sticks. "Sure. Just help me with the lights first."

Fish glanced around. "This place has lights?"

"Sort of." She sat cross-legged on the floor and opened her bag, freeing Fulton (letting the cat out of the bag, as it were). He proceeded to survey the fifth floor, his head high, his tail scattering dust motes every which way as he set off in search of those rats she'd mentioned.

Dory extracted the kerosene lantern and set it in front of her while she ferreted for the Zippo lighter.

"Where'd you get that?" Fish asked.

"Mr. Zuk." She raised the globe to access the wick, thumbed a flame from the Zippo, and set the lantern ablaze. "Now the candles," she said, indicating the sconces on the walls.

They removed the hurricanes, blew off the dust, and lit the ancient stubs.

"These won't last very long," Fish remarked.

Dory went to her bag again and held it open for his inspection.

"Well, for Pete's sake," he whispered, peering at the pile of candles. "You really did think of everything, Dor." He cleared his throat. "I won't doubt you again."

Dory grinned. "You probably should," she said, then swept her arm toward room 7 to indicate their sleeping quarters. "Unless everybody wants their own floor?"

"No way," Pike said.

"You've got to be putting me on," Fish echoed.

They pulled the covers off the ghost chairs. Dory removed the dust-furred quilt from the bed to reveal a worn but functional mattress. "There's a wardrobe on the fourth floor," she said. "The doors have been closed all these years, so the linens inside are pretty clean."

Fish was still unwilling to brave the dumbwaiter alone, so Dory made the trip, retrieving the dustpan and broom from the second-floor storage room and a pile of linens from the fourth-floor wardrobe. Back in room 7, she pulled the portable radio from her bag and switched it on. Pike set to sweeping. Dory dusted the sconces and brought the candles to life. Fish beat the mattress with the broom handle, then made the bed with the clean linens.

It was past midnight when they finally sat for a rest in the ghost chairs.

Fish wiped sweat from his brow, leaving a streak of grime.

Dory rolled up her sleeves a few turns, aware of the stagnant press of the room, which hadn't known fresh air in fifty-five years. She looked at the windows. If they could get one open, perhaps it would let in a draft, even with the boards covering the outside.

Crossing to the one on the right and releasing its latch, she positioned the heels of her hands under the sash and pushed. It gave easily, letting in a distinct scent of decay from the rotted boards. She poked the planks. After years and years in the damp, salty air, they felt pliant. Through the gaps, she could see enough of the street below to know that it was empty.

She looked at her brothers. "The fish market's vacant. Do you think anybody would notice if we just kicked out one or two of the boards?"

Pike shook his head. "People mostly look down, not up."

(Which says an awful lot about people, doesn't it?)

Fish rolled his eyes. "Dor, we can't just—" He stopped. Gave her a long look.

Dory smiled pointedly at him. "Can't just what?"

A grin bloomed on Fish's face. "Nothing."

Standing on the window seat, Dory chose an especially weathered-looking plank and took aim. With her brothers supporting her from behind, she landed a good, solid kick, releasing two boards with a satisfying crunch. As the wood gave way and fell toward South Street, the Byrnes crowded into the alcove and peeked through the newly made hole just in time to see the wood splinter on the pavement below with a terrific crash. In the distance, a dog barked at the ruckus, but it seemed that the rest of Lower Manhattan hadn't noticed a thing.

A glorious breeze, ripe with the seaport's brine, filtered in. Dory, Fish, and Pike dragged the bed to the window and lay head-to-head-to-head, gazing out at the East River. Fulton joined them. The storm had passed, and the sky was full of stars now. A million pinpricks of light reflected in the river's inky blackness.

"It's a waterfront apartment," Fish whispered. "A penthouse, even."

Dory nudged her head against his. "And a secret one."

The three of them flipped onto their backs. They found that if they positioned themselves just so, all they could see was sky. This was a thrilling perspective for three children who had lived all their lives in a city—wondrous though it may have been—where the sky was never entirely visible from one's bed, always blocked by one building or another. The moon felt somehow nearby, as if they could warm their hands on its glow if they only reached toward it.

Dory thought of Pop. She wondered what time it was for him right now, and whether he had the same grand view of the nearly full moon.

They closed their eyes for a moment. Just to rest them.

And the next thing any of them knew, they'd spent the night in the old hotel.

✳

Caputo's was closed for the weekend, but even if it hadn't been, the Byrnes could have shouted and stomped and turned the radio up as loud as they wanted. On the fifth floor of the old hotel, there were two whole stories between them and the rest of the world, so there was no more tippy-toeing around in fear of being discovered.

It was delightful, the not tippy-toeing. Tippy-toeing is exhausting.

Fish took the filthy cover off the card table and wadded it up in the corner while Pike dusted the chairs. Dory retrieved plates from the second floor and laid out crullers and 7UPs from home for breakfast. She set the kerosene lamp in the center of the table. The boards she'd kicked out of the window in room 7 only let in dusty shafts of light.

Fish took a swig of his soda. "What should we do? Explore?"

"We've gotta clean this place up," Dory said, putting her feet on the table. "We can explore as we go. Just don't expect to find anything. I already took the good stuff. The picture frame and the dime Pike sent to Captain America. That's it. Otherwise, it's all just old junk."

(Other than the diamond, of course.)

Fish stifled a belch. "Right. Let's clean up."

They started with the beds. Cramming into the big

one in room 7 had been all right for one night, but none of them wanted to make a habit out of it. Together, they inspected the beds on the third and fourth floors. Serviceable, but too big to fit in the dumbwaiter. So, Fish took apart two of the frames with a screwdriver they found in the storage room, while Dory and Pike dragged the mattresses into the hall and beat them with a broom handle. Back in room 7, they left the big bed where it was and reassembled the others by the window on the right.

Next, they reviewed the old hotel's remaining linens, sorting them into two piles: those peppered with rat droppings and those that could be salvaged. Fish held his nose and stuffed the filthy ones into a corner to dispose of later. The others they hauled down to wash in Caputo's kitchen, its sinks significantly roomier than the one in the third floor's tiny water closet.

Dory found a box of soap flakes. "Think Mr. Caputo will be sore if we use just a little?"

Fish raised one eyebrow. "If Mr. Caputo ever finds out about all this, I don't think it's the soap flakes he's going to be sore about."

They plugged the sinks, dumped in the linens, and added a sprinkling of soap to each. Pike, too short to help, sat on the countertop petting the cat.

They scrubbed and wrung, then heaved the load into lobster pots to haul back to the third floor, where they draped everything over chairs to drip dry.

They would need to bring pillows from home for sleeping. The old hotel's pillows smelled like ancient mildew

160

but would make fine cushions for the window seats in the big bedroom. The children collected the least offensive specimens in a pile on the floor of the lobby to beat the mustiness out of them.

Dory picked up the top one, then retrieved the portable radio and tuned it to WNYC, which just happened to be playing "Pistol Packin' Mama." She nodded. "Perfect."

"Perfect for what?" Fish said.

Dory wound up and swung for his head. A direct hit.

The pillow spat a cloud of dust into the murky kerosene light as a wide grin spread over Fish's face. He lunged for a pillow of his own.

But not as quickly as Pike did. The younger Byrnes proceeded to gang up on the oldest, showing no mercy as they rained blows from both sides.

"Hey," Fish shouted, hardly able to speak. "That's two against one! No fair!" He leaped behind the reception desk to defend himself as Dory fought with a pillow in each hand, spinning like a top and battering her brothers in turns. Pike's size limited his range, but he quickly took advantage of the rolling piano stool, which allowed him to sneak in and attack from the side.

Fish lost his grip on his pillow and scrambled around the reception desk to collect it, which gave Dory the opportunity to tackle him. Pike sat on Fish's legs, and he and Dory pummeled their brother until he begged for mercy.

Fulton watched the action from the safety of the room 1 cubbyhole, surveying the battle with the sort of disdain that only a cat can aspire to.

They gave up, laughing and panting, as a haze of dust settled around them. It was the most legendary pillow fight ever known in the city of New York. Maybe even the whole state.

Dory sprawled on the floor of the lobby. Fish sprawled next to her.

Pike wormed his way between them, cuddling under Fish's armpit. "I like it here."

Fish poked Dory in the ribs. "I do too."

His grin was the widest she'd seen on his face since November.

✳

That first weekend, the dingy old hotel got a lot less dingy.

They set cushions in the window seats. They made Fulton a litter box out of a desk drawer and some ashes from the potbellied stove. They swept and they polished, set new candles in sconces, hauled buckets of water from Caputo's kitchen, and cleaned five decades' worth of grime from the windows. At night, they dumped rotted quilts and mouse droppings into the trash bin in the alley.

Wiping out the cubbyholes, Pike came upon Mae's letter to Chester and tossed it in the trash pile by the dumbwaiter.

"Hey!" Dory shouted. "That's not trash!" She picked up the yellowed envelope and clasped it to her ribs with both hands.

"What is it?" Pike asked.

"It's a letter."

"Duh," Pike said. "What's it say?"

"None of your business," Dory replied, feeling unaccountably protective of Mae and Chester. She headed for the dumbwaiter. "I'll be back in a sec."

The scrap of poem was still in the desk drawer in room 6. Dory removed the brittle paper and ran a finger over Chester's scrawl: *My Beloved Mae.* She read again the fading words: "As to me I know of nothing else but miracles." She nestled the poem fragment against Mae's letter, then tucked the envelope back in the drawer. Dory couldn't say what the poem meant, or why whoever wrote it hadn't even bothered to make it rhyme. All she knew was that she needed Chester and Mae to be together. It felt important, somehow.

*

On Sunday night, they heated up a can of pork and beans in one of Mr. Caputo's stockpots. Dory shuffled the deck of cards, and they played Hearts while they ate.

Fish played the seven of diamonds. "I hate leaving you two alone here tomorrow while I'm at the Navy Yard."

Dory shrugged. "Better here than the apartment." She laid down a nine and took the trick.

"That's for sure," Fish said. "But still."

"Do you have to go, Fish?" Pike said.

"'Course he has to. He's a grown-up, remember?" Dory looked at Fish pointedly. "Isn't that what you said, Fish? That you're a grown-up?"

Fish only rolled his eyes.

Dory played the king of clubs. "Grown-ups have jobs."

"It'll be a job someday," Fish said. "For now, it's only an apprenticeship."

Pike played a four. "What's the difference?"

Fish pulled a card from his hand. "Jobs pay money. Apprenticeships don't." He laid a jack on the table. "I'll put everything the way it was on the second floor, but don't use the dumbwaiter unless Caputo's is either still closed or already real busy, okay? Otherwise somebody might hear you."

Pike and Dory nodded.

"And you know I can't come back until Mr. Caputo rolls in the awning, right?"

Pike frowned. "I wish there was another way in and out."

Dory thought about this. "What about the window in room three?"

Fish wrinkled one side of his nose. "What about it?"

"It's missing most of its boards," she said. "And the only window beneath it is in the second-floor storage room. Below that, Caputo's kitchen's only got one, and it's at least twelve or fourteen feet farther down the alley. If we rigged some sort of a ladder—"

"No way," Fish said.

"Why not?"

Fish sighed.

"Don't sigh like that, Fish," Dory said. "That's what the old Fish would do. The one from before. You're the new Fish."

"Yeah, well, old me or new me, nobody's climbing out a third-story window."

"Why not?" Dory asked again.

"Because it's dangerous."

"Not if we made a really good ladder."

Fish shook his head in exasperation. "Besides, what if somebody saw you?"

"It's an alley," Dory said. "The building across is boarded up just like this one. And I'd look both ways."

"I said no, Dor."

Dory crossed her arms over her chest.

"Dor?"

"What?"

"I said no."

Dory heaved a sigh of her own. "I heard you."

But hearing Fish, Dory reasoned, was very different from listening to him.

TWO
PICKLES

Fish left early on Monday.

Dory and Pike spent the morning exploring. Down below, Caputo's opened for business around ten, so they steered clear of the dumbwaiter until then, when they figured its groaning would be drowned out by the restaurant's din.

Pike found the cloak in the wardrobe in room 1 and put it on, giving his best Count Dracula impression. Which was not an impressive impression at all, as far as Dory was concerned. He looked nothing like Bela Lugosi in *The Return of the Vampire* or Lon Chaney in *Son of Dracula*. Vampires had fangs, for starters. Pike still didn't even have a whole mouthful of teeth, let alone extra.

They found a set of dominoes under the bed in room 2 and built a run from one end of the lobby to the other, sending Fulton skittering when they knocked it down.

They steered clear of room 5, which had gashes in its

walls, and what may or may not have been a bullet hole in its wardrobe.

In room 4, they found an old dime museum pamphlet wedged between the bed and the wall. "Monthly Catalogue: Eden Musee," it read. They sat on the bare mattress to page through the museum's offerings. Séances. A waxworks. A chamber of horrors.

The Byrnes had been to a dime museum once—last year, Pop had taken them to see Professor Heckler's Flea Circus at Hubert's Museum on Forty-Second Street. The museum had other attractions besides the fleas, of course, but most of them were frightening. Not the good sort of frightening, like monster movies, but the sad and troublesome sort. Tattooed ladies and real, live skeleton people and such. Pop had steered the three of them past those cruelties.

But the flea circus. That was something else. Professor Heckler had trained his fleas to pull tiny cannons and chariots, to roll miniature balls with their feet, to turn minuscule carousels. He took each of the performers out of a cotton-lined box with a pair of tweezers to do its trick. When Professor Heckler asked for a volunteer to feed the creatures, Dory's hand shot up of its own accord. He lined them up on her arm and let them drink their fill. She had worn the itchy bites on her forearm like a badge of honor all that week.

Tucked into the center of the Eden Musee pamphlet was a postcard advertising a fortune teller.

Pike shook his head. "I thought you said there was nothing good in this place." He paused. "Madam Luna," he read. "Knows all. Sees all. Tells all."

Between the pamphlet's pages was a worn and faded card bearing a yellow sun with a mysterious face. A fortune teller's card.

Pike looked from left to right, right to left, surveying room 4. "Madam Luna?" he whispered. "Was this your room?"

Madam Luna did not reply.

✳

They wrote to Pop, though it was a little hard to come up with material.

"We can't tell him about this place, can we?" Pike asked.

Dory looked at him like he was off his nut. "Of course we can't. *Make it cheerful*, remember?"

"This place is cheerful," Pike said. "This place is swell."

"It is swell," Dory agreed. "But it's also secret. Which is part of what makes it swell."

"Well, what should I write about, then?"

Dory considered this. "Tell him about the last day of school. Tell him about your report card. How Mrs. Denton rated you satisfactory on every single thing. Even posture. Even cleanliness."

Pike shrugged. "Satisfactory isn't so great."

"It's the highest mark they've got in the second grade."

Pike looked at her. "Did Miss Ozinskas rate you satisfactory on everything?"

Dory scowled at him. "There was some room for improvement."

They took the dumbwaiter to the fifth floor and played
billiards, setting the kerosene lamp in the middle of the
table and working around it. After Pike won the fifth
game in a row, Dory decided she didn't like billiards.

She also decided she was hungry.

"What would you like for lunch, Pike? If you could
have anything?"

"There's peanut butter," he said. "And apples."

"I didn't ask what we have. I asked what you'd wish for."

Pike didn't even have to think about it. "That's easy.
Pastrami on rye with a pickle."

Dory gave a smile best described as mildly sinister.
"All right."

"You brought pickles?"

"No, but I know where we could get some."

Pike squinted at her.

She grabbed the portable radio and fifty cents from
the mayonnaise jar. "Come with me."

"You're supposed to ask Fish before you take money
out of the jar." Pike picked up Fulton and followed.

Dory ignored the chiding. She ushered him into the
dumbwaiter and hauled them down to the wardrobe on
the fourth floor.

"What are we doing?" he asked.

Dory grabbed a pile of bedsheets. "Getting supplies."

"Supplies for what?"

"You'll see."

They continued to the third floor, to room 3. The eye glared at them from above the door as they entered.

Dory laid the sheets on the bed, then looked at the window appraisingly. Its missing boards had left a perfect escape hatch.

"What are you doing?" Pike's tone suggested that he knew exactly what Dory was doing.

She wedged her fingers into the groove in the bottom rail and raised the window.

"Dory, Fish said no."

She unfurled two of the bedsheets. "Fish isn't here."

Twisting the sheets at their ends, she wished she'd paid more attention when Pop talked about which knots were best for which jobs. Though she was pretty sure he'd never mentioned anything about the best knot for tying sheets together into a ladder that would let you lower yourself out the third-floor window of an abandoned hotel without smashing your head open like a pumpkin.

"Dory."

"What?" She tugged on the knot as hard as she could, tightening it into a rock-hard ball. "Do you want a pastrami on rye and a pickle, or don't you?"

Pike crossed his arms over his chest. "I don't."

"Come on, Pike. I don't feel like peanut butter." She unfurled another sheet.

"Fish said it's dangerous."

"He said the same thing about the dumbwaiter."

"Yeah, but—" A shadow of understanding passed over Pike's face. "You're not gonna leave me here, are you?"

She looked at him. "You have to stay here to throw the ladder down to me when I get back with the sandwiches. We can't just leave it hanging out there for everybody to see."

His eyes filled. "But, Dory—"

Dory tightened the next knot. "Look, Pike. I'm about to get you the biggest, saltiest, most perfect pickle on the Lower East Side. It's going to be great, okay?"

He sniffled. "What am I supposed to do while you're gone?"

She turned on the radio. Fats Waller was singing "Ain't Misbehavin'."

Which . . . well.

"*Perry Mason*'s on in ten minutes," Dory said.

Pike stroked Fulton's tail. "Will you be back before *Perry Mason*'s over?"

She nodded. "The deli's only four blocks."

Pike tapped his foot. He narrowed his eyes at her. "Two pickles."

"Fine. Two pickles." Dory extended a hand to shake on it.

She tied one end of the bedsheet ladder to the leg of the massive wardrobe, then peeked out the window ever so tentatively, just in case anybody lurking in the alley below (because lurking is something people do in alleys) happened to look up and see a twelve-year-old in the window of a hotel that had been empty for more than fifty years.

There were no lurkers. Only the trash-littered ground below.

Which was farther away than she'd imagined.

Dory lowered the sheet ladder out the window and looked at Pike. "Pull it back in once I'm down, and then keep an eye out for me, okay? And think of that pickle."

"Pickles." Pike emphasized the *s*. "Two pickles."

"Right." Dory checked both ways again, then took a seat on the window frame and slid her feet through, flipping onto her stomach and grabbing the first knot with both hands. She winked at Pike. "Easy peasy." Loosening her grip on the knot, she let herself slide. Not for the first time, she was glad to be in trousers.

She lowered herself in a stop-start way until she connected with the next knot. That brought her nearly to the window of the second-floor storage room. *Please,* she thought, *don't let there be anybody in there.* Surely nobody would need tomatoes at this hour, would they? She felt the window ledge with her toes and rested on it for a moment.

Poised in midair, she heard a voice below her. A rumbling Italian bass. Mr. Caputo.

Apparently, somebody did need tomatoes.

Dory looked up to see Pike's anxious face assessing her progress.

"Why are you stopping?" he whispered.

She grimaced. "Mr. Caputo's in there," she whispered back.

Pike's eyebrows met in the middle, just like Fish's. He peered down at the bedsheets dangling below Dory's feet, smack in the middle of the storage room window. "Move the sheet rope!" he hissed.

Dory used one foot to flick the ladder's tail to the side of the window frame, then tightened her grip on the bedsheet and prepared to stay a while.

To hang out, quite literally.

Sweat prickled across her forehead.

She closed her eyes, picturing the sandwich menu at Aaronson's. As the muffled muttering and clanking of Mr. Caputo continued below her, she decided on an egg salad with lettuce and tomato on pumpernickel.

She looked both ways. Still nobody on either side of the alley.

Her hands burned something awful. Her arms felt like they might just come loose at the shoulders. Wedged against the bricks, her toes were starting to go numb. And worst of all, she felt a thoroughly inconvenient sneeze coming.

Hitching her nose back and forth, Dory scrunched her eyes shut. Hitched her nose some more, willing it to behave. But it seemed determined to betray her. She gripped the sheet ladder as tight as she could with her sweating palms and braced herself.

The mighty sneeze thundered its way out, echoing in the alley. Two more followed, each louder than the next, each loosening her grip on the bedsheet just a little bit more.

"Dory, be quiet!" Pike whispered. "Somebody'll hear you!"

She shot him a withering stare and gritted her teeth, waiting for Mr. Caputo to stick his head out the window to investigate the ruckus. Her mind raced to find a plausible explanation for her current position.

From inside Caputo's storage room, the muffled sounds continued. Had Mr. Caputo really not heard? Dory's nose was dripping, but letting go of the ladder to swipe at it wasn't an option. Her grip was barely holding out as it was.

It felt like an eternity before the noise from the second floor subsided enough that Dory thought it might be safe to lower herself past the window. She was certain her palms must be bloodied by now as she slid herself down to the next knot, squinting into the storage room.

It was blessedly empty.

Sweat leaking into her eyes, she juddered herself the rest of the way down, reaching the last knot and then letting go, trusting gravity. She landed with a thud, stretched her hands, swiped at her nose with her sleeve, and gave Pike a panting thumbs-up.

He glared down at her from the third-floor window, holding up two fingers to remind her of his order.

Dory sprinted straight for Pearl Street. For Aaronson's Delicatessen.

✳

Pike was waiting at the window when she returned.

Perry Mason had already cracked the case, but just one bite of pickle made him forget about being angry.

And if you're figuring that Dory learned from the sheet ladder incident and never again lowered herself out the window for an egg salad sandwich, you'd be figuring wrong.

LIKE ANY
OTHER
THURSDAY

The old hotel proved a perfect hideout.

Fish went to the Navy Yard.

Dory and Pike stayed hidden.

(Mostly.)

But there were some logistics to work out. Thursday evenings, for example.

Thursday evenings were a challenge because the Byrnes were expected at dinner downstairs in the restaurant. And this is probably stating the obvious, but they were expected to arrive through the front door.

"Wouldn't Mr. Caputo be surprised if we just stepped out of the dumbwaiter while he was getting oyster crackers from the storage room?" Pike said.

Fish gave a dark chuckle. "*Surprised* is one word for it."

"We're running low on food anyhow," Dory said. "And I want some stuff from the apartment."

"Yeah," Pike agreed. "I need more underwear."

Dory wrinkled her nose. She looked at Fish. "Me and Pike will do a supply run tomorrow while you're at the Yard."

"Pike and I," Pike corrected.

Dory stuck her tongue out at him, then looked back at Fish. "We'll leave with you in the morning, run the errands, and figure on someplace to hide before we meet you at the pier for dinner at Caputo's."

Fish crossed his arms over his chest, pondering.

"Even if tomorrow wasn't a Thursday, we can't stay locked up all summer, Fish," Dory said. "We're going to have to go out sometimes." She saw that the groove of worry had returned to his forehead. "But we'll be careful."

Fish looked at her. "Really careful?"

Dory nodded. "Really careful."

＊

They left early.

Dory and Pike said goodbye to Fish at the docks and walked north on Pearl Street.

At the corner of Catherine and Madison, they looked both ways. No sign of Reedy. No sign of any net-wielding foundling-catchers. They crept up the fire escape stairs and opened the apartment window as quietly as they could.

"Let's just get what we need and get out of here, okay?" Dory whispered.

They found a duffel bag in Pop's closet and crammed

it full of pillows, clothes, and what was left of the food in the cupboard:

- An unopened box of Rice Krispies
- Two cans of evaporated milk
- One can of Green Giant corn niblets
- Half a package of sugar
- Four boxes of macaroni and cheese
- A tin of sardines (several years old, for Fulton)
- A dusty box of lime Jell-O

They hauled the duffel bag out the window together, Pike pulling, Dory pushing.

"If Mrs. Kopek stops us," Dory said, "just tell her we're staying at a friend's apartment this weekend."

Pike nodded, then opened his eyes wide, remembering something. "My library books!" He started back into the apartment.

"Leave them, Pike."

He looked stricken. "But they're due back. I'll get in trouble."

Dory thought to tell her brother that the library was probably low on the list of city institutions they needed to worry about right now, but Pike had already disappeared into the apartment. He emerged a moment later with a stack of books.

Dory unzipped the duffel and stowed them, rolling her eyes at her brother. Rolling her eyes at her brother so dramatically, in fact, that she neglected to re-zip the duffel all the way. The opening she left was big enough that, as she rounded the corner on the third-floor landing and shifted the bag to her other shoulder, the can of corn niblets broke free and hit the iron grate with a resounding clank, then started rolling.

Toward Mr. Kowalczyk's open window.

The same window where he always sat.

The same window where he was sitting now.

Dory watched the Jolly Green Giant turn lolloping cartwheels across the fire escape grate, then come to a stop under his window. In the background, the Tsitak twins' wailing could be heard from apartment 4.

Mr. Kowalczyk looked down at the can, then up at Dory.

Her eyes wide, she stepped forward and bent to retrieve it, her face only inches from the recluse now. It was the closest she'd ever been to him. It was close enough to see the graying hairs sprouting from his chin. Close enough to see that his red-rimmed eyes looked wary.

Close enough that as the half-used sack of sugar tipped out of the still-open bag, it fell through the window and landed upside-down in Mr. Kowalczyk's lap, dousing him in Domino's.

From behind her, Dory could hear Pike's sharp inhale, mirroring her own.

None of them moved for what felt like an eternity.

Not Dory. Not Pike. Not Mr. Kowalczyk.

"Jeez, sir," Dory said at last. Her voice was a pinched whisper. "I'm real sorry."

Mr. Kowalczyk said nothing. He didn't even look at her. He only stared down at the quarter inch of granulated sugar decorating his knees and cascading onto the floor of apartment 3.

Surveying the sugary carnage, Dory weighed their options. Should they stand their ground and face the recluse's wrath, or leave their worldly belongings on the third-floor landing and make a run for it while there was still time?

But as she contemplated their escape, Mr. Kowalczyk began calmly and carefully brushing the spilled sugar from his lap into the Domino's sack. She and Pike stood there on the fire escape grate, their mouths hanging open, while Mr. Kowalczyk folded the top of the bag three times over.

He held it out to Dory. "You'll want to zip that duffel up tight now."

"Yes, sir," Dory whispered. She nestled the sugar between the cans of evaporated milk and tugged hard on the zipper. "Thanks."

He blinked twice, nodded, and looked away.

✳

Having learned a valuable lesson about the unwieldy nature of canned goods, Dory and Pike had to find someplace they could spend the day without lugging the duffel around. They returned the library books, then decided to take in a double feature at the Century: *Going My Way*, which was Pike's choice because it had Bing Crosby, and *The Lady and the Monster*, which was Dory's because it had a mind-controlling brain in a jar. Ernest Klein had seen it already and told her that the jar got smashed at the end, splattering brain juice all over. Ernest had kind of ruined the ending, but Dory wanted to see the brain juice for herself anyhow.

She approached the woman in the ticket cage and slipped fifty cents through the slot. "Two tickets to *The Lady and the Monster*, please."

The ticket woman was reading *Modern Screen* and didn't look up as she slid the tickets over the counter. Her long, sharp fingernails were painted cotton-candy pink.

"But, Dory," Pike said, "I thought we going to see two pict—"

Dory coughed into her hand and nudged Pike away from the ticket lady. She steered him around the cage and into the theater lobby, her mouth watering at the thick scent of butter.

Pike squinted up at her. "Why are you shoving me? And why didn't you get tickets for the Bing Crosby picture?"

"Shh!" She looked over both shoulders. "Fish would be proud of us. We're saving money."

"Saving money?" Pike cocked his head, eyes still narrowed. "You mean stealing?"

Dory rolled her eyes. "Sticking around for a second picture isn't stealing." She grabbed him by the hand and led him down the carpeted hall.

"It is so," Pike whispered. "It's stealing from Bing Crosby."

Dory pushed open the door to theater 1. "Bing makes loads of money. He doesn't need fifty cents from a couple of kids. And besides, Bing would want us to see his movie."

"I think Bing would want to send you straight to jail on Rikers Island." Pike sighed, resigned to his sister's life of crime. "Can we sit in the balcony?"

"Sure." Dory let go of his hand to haul the duffel up the stairs.

They got seats in the front row as the lights dimmed and the newsreel began, all patriotic music, horns, and marching, then airplane engines and gunfire as the screen flickered with footage from the D-Day invasions. The announcer described four thousand naval ships landing troops on Hitler's doorstep. Soldier after soldier marched across the screen in black and white.

Dory knew it was dumb as anything, but she poked Pike in the ribs. "Look for Pop."

He had his ears covered against the roar of the guns, but he nodded anyhow, never taking his eyes off the screen as the newsreel showed footage of men being carried off the beach on stretchers.

Dory shook her head at how something so impossibly far away could feel so impossibly close.

The stirring music resumed as a beaming American soldier held up a captured Nazi flag. The announcer said the soldier would use it as a doormat when he got back home.

With that, the newsreel ended, "Yankee Doodle" trumpeting in the background.

Pike took his hands away from his ears and looked at Dory. "I didn't see him."

"Me neither."

Pike leaned his head back. "Do you think Pop will bring home a Nazi flag to use as a doormat?"

Dory nodded. "Probably."

The theater went dark as the projectionist changed out the newsreel for the feature.

"Dory?" Pike whispered.

"Yeah?"

He reached for her hand. "I don't really think Bing Crosby would want to send you to Rikers."

Dory squeezed her brother's fingers as the feature began. She held on to them until long after the credits had rolled.

✳

They met Fish on the waterfront as his ferry returned from the Navy Yard across the river in Brooklyn. He was practically giddy with the day's newfound knowledge. The business of the harbor bustled by as the Byrnes sat on an upturned crate, listening to Fish wax poetic about hulls and horsepower, bulkheads and berths, and enjoying the free show of the fish market. Longshoremen, their sunbaked arms thick and sinewy, hefted barrels into trucks. Their overalls were filmed with scales and oil, and they whistled and sang while they worked. Pike giggled when one of them sang a song about kissing.

Dory was too old to giggle about kissing.

Fish nudged Pike, pointing out a man in an eye patch carrying a crate of live lobsters.

When he saw Pike gawking, the man veered their way. "Want to see them?" His voice rumbled like a storm on the sea. Setting down his load, he began extricating himself from a net slung over his shoulders.

Pike watched, breathless, as the creatures in the crate squirmed and writhed, their claws massive and terrifying.

Caught in his own net like a fly in a spider's web, the man muttered a word that would have had Dory clapping erasers for weeks if Miss O'Donnell had heard her say it. "Useless as a chocolate teapot," the man said, dropping the net to the ground at last.

Dory eyed it. "What are you gonna do with that?"

The man kicked the coils at his feet. "Toss it in the harbor and let it sink for all the good it's doing. The thing's shot. Catch just swims right on through."

"Are you really going to throw it out?" Dory asked.

Fish looked at her quizzically.

"Why?" the man asked. "You collecting nets for the war effort or something?"

Dory squinted at him. "Yes." It was true in a way, she supposed.

The man gathered up the damp coils and handed them over. "It's yours, then."

"Jeez, thanks, mister." Dory blinked at their good fortune. She would stow the netting in the alley to retrieve later.

"You're welcome." The man adjusted his eye patch, then turned his head to hawk and spit into the harbor.

"Swell," Pike whispered.

The lobsterman winked.

At least, that's how Dory interpreted it. It was hard to tell.

✳

They arrived at Caputo's a little after seven. Just like any other Thursday, the bell above the door announced their arrival. Just like any other Thursday, they took their seats at the table by the window. And just like any other Thursday, Mr. Caputo shouted "Bambini!" from behind the bar, then came out to greet them. He touched Dory's cheek with two fingers, chucked Pike under the chin, and shook Fish's hand.

"Any word from your papa since the invasion?"

They answered with shakes of their heads.

Mr. Caputo grunted. "It's okay. He's okay. Everything's okay."

The three of them nodded.

Mr. Caputo crossed his arms over his chest. His preposterous eyebrows met in the middle as he looked at Dory. "You sleeping over, bambina?"

Dory felt all the blood drain out of her face.

How could he possibly have guessed?

Had someone seen them?

Had they left something amiss in the storage room?

"We're, uh..." She glanced at Fish, her eyes wide.

Fish inclined his head toward the duffel bag by her feet. "He means the bag you packed. You know. For your sleepover at Rosemary's."

Dory glanced down as understanding dawned. "Oh." She looked at Mr. Caputo and gave a shaky laugh. "Right. I'm going to my friend's after dinner."

A crash drew Mr. Caputo's attention. He muttered something in Italian, then shouted to the Byrnes as he disappeared into the kitchen. "I'll be back in a minute!"

Dory let out a long, low whistle. She shoved the duffel under the table, then looked at Fish. "A sleepover at Rosemary's? You thought that one up pretty quick."

Fish gave her a sideways smile. "I learned from the master."

WHEN IT
CAME TO
HAPPY ENDINGS

The lobsterman's netting may have been useless for catching shad, but cut and tied properly, it made an excellent set of hammocks. The children hung these by the windows in the fourth-floor lobby, fastening them to exposed studs on one side and wrought iron candle sconces on the other. The netting turned the room into a sort of pirate's retreat. It rained on and off for most of the next week, and Dory and Pike logged hours and hours in the makeshift bunks.

On Wednesday morning, Pike lay in one of the nets, poring over the newspaper Fish had brought back the day before. Dory sat on the floor with a paring knife and a framed portrait—an angry-looking, bearded man in a gold-buttoned military uniform—that they'd found behind the chess table.

Pike looked up from page 13. "There's a lot more names

from the European area," he said. *The New York Times* regularly listed locals wounded and missing. In today's edition, the casualties were just above an advertisement for Crisco:

9 OUT OF 10 DOCTORS SAY:

"It's Digestible!"

Which didn't seem like much of an endorsement.

Dory shook her head. "Why are you looking at that, Pike?"

He widened his eyes as if the answer should be obvious. "Checking for Pop."

Dory set down the paring knife. "Pop's not on the list." She knew Pop wasn't on the list because she'd already checked. She always checked. "If Pop was on the list, that wouldn't be the first we'd hear about it. We'd get a telegram."

The War Department sent telegrams to notify families when a soldier was missing, injured, or dead. "Regret to inform you," they began. Or so Dory had heard. Western Union delivered them. Nobody wanted a visit from the Western Union man.

Pike sighed. "Fine." He turned the page. "I'll do the crossword, then."

"Nobody can do the crossword. It's impossible."

"No it isn't." He ran his finger down the list of clues for a moment, looking up with a grin. "Told you. Fifteen across is *sarcophagus*."

Dory gave a blank stare. That sounded like a made-up word.

"It's a coffin for mummies," Pike said. "I learned it on our museum field trip last year."

"Mm," Dory murmured. On her own class trip to the Metropolitan Museum of Art a few years ago, she'd never gotten that far. She'd lagged behind her group in the arms and armor wing, which included an excellent exhibit of armored horses. A dozen or more of them, all in parade formation. They weren't real horses or anything, so what possible harm could a second-grader do by putting a foot into one of the stirrups and swinging herself into the saddle?

Apparently, the museum staff thought it could be quite a lot of harm. Dory was apprehended by a guard after only just catching a glimpse of the view from the noble steed's back. She spent the rest of the field trip doing forced labor behind the information desk in the lobby and missed the mummies altogether. Which was a shame. But worth it, in retrospect.

"I'm done," she said, holding up the portrait for Pike to see.

"What are we going to do with that anyway?"

Dory held the portrait to her face. The eye holes matched perfectly. "Try it," she said, handing it to him.

"It's swell, Dory," Pike said. "But what's it for?"

She grinned. "Come with me."

✳

Which was how a whole pot of macaroni and cheese got splattered all over the fifth-floor lobby.

When Fish got back that night, he let himself in through the kitchen window and boiled up a box of Kraft, fresh from the market, then hauled the steaming pot to the fifth floor.

Exiting the dumbwaiter, he noticed the portrait right away. It looked nice, he thought, where Dory and Pike had hung it. Behind the billiard table, neatly covering one of the spots where the holes in the plaster were so big, they revealed the ancient building's innards.

"Dory?" he called. "Pike?"

He heard Pike giggle from room 7 and crossed to the bedroom, keeping his eyes on the portrait. It seemed to be keeping its eyes on him as well. Portraits did that sometimes, he'd heard. But this one...He moved left. The eyes followed him in the flickering candlelight. He stopped. The eyes stopped, too.

Fish held his breath and crept back toward room 7.

Had the portrait just blinked? "Dory? Pike?" he whispered.

A voice hissed from the painting. "Fiiiiissshhh..."

The pot of macaroni and cheese clattered to the floor, sending their dinner oozing all over the rough wood planks.

Dory stepped out from a hole in the wall, just to the left of the portrait.

Fish exhaled. "Jeez Louise, Dory."

Pike emerged from room 7, cackling. He took in the mess approvingly. "This place just keeps getting better."

✳

On Thursday morning, Dory and Pike left the old hotel with Fish again. Waving goodbye at the pier, they munched on orange slices for breakfast and watched the ferry cut its way across the river. The weather had turned, leaving the city steaming. It had made their decision about how to spend the day an easy one.

From June until September, anyone who was anyone on the Lower East Side went to the Hamilton Fish Park Municipal Swimming Pool at Pitt and Houston. On any given summer day, the place swarmed with students from PS 42. Even the teachers went to the municipal pool, though it was awkward seeing teachers in bathing suits.

Dory and Pike got there as the manager unlocked the gate. Arriving early allowed them to stake out a spot before the pool deck got packed. Pike chose a space near the wall so his book wouldn't get splashed.

Dory shook her head. "What kind of a crumb brings a book to the pool, anyhow?"

"I'm on the last chapter." Pike unfurled his towel.

Dory laid hers next to his, then went to change into her swimming suit.

Maeve Morrison and Evie Sullivan were leaving the bathroom as she arrived. They hugged like long-lost friends even though they'd only just seen each other the Friday before last.

Dory looked down at Maeve's and Evie's swimsuits. They were both wearing two-pieces that showed their belly buttons.

Evie caught Dory's glance. She covered her navel with both hands. "I can't go out there."

Maeve rolled her eyes. "Honestly, Evie." She looked at Dory. "I keep telling her she looks swell. Doesn't she look swell, Dory?"

Dory cocked her head to one side. She didn't have much of an opinion one way or the other, except that:

1. She was glad to be wearing a one-piece herself.
2. If Evie was going to spend the whole day covering up her stomach with her hands, there didn't seem to be much point to wearing a two-piece, did there?

"Sure," she said. "You look swell, Evie."

Evie's hands fluttered away from her midriff. "Any word from your pop, Dory?"

"Not for a few weeks."

"Me neither," Evie said. "But Maeve's dad is coming home."

"Really?" An ugly knot of jealousy tightened in Dory's stomach.

"He was wounded," Maeve said. "He's not able to fight anymore."

The knot loosened. "Jeez, Maeve. That's...I guess that's good?" Dory's sentence rose in a question mark. When it came to happy endings, it seemed everyone's standards had changed.

Maeve's eyes went swimmy. She lowered her voice to a whisper. "He lost his left hand."

"Oh." Dory didn't know what to say. Hadn't they only been talking about bikini bathing suits a moment ago? The world had become a series of strange and awful juxtapositions. "Still, Maeve, I'm happy for you that he's coming home."

"Me too," Maeve said. She sniffled. "Anyhow, see you in the water." She and Evie waved and headed down the stairs toward the crowded pool deck.

Dory chose a changing stall, latched the door behind her, and sat down on the bench inside. Her head was spinning with the sorts of questions better left unasked. If it meant Pop could come home tomorrow, would Dory want him wounded? Would she wish for him to lose a hand? Both hands? A foot? She put her head against the stall's plywood side and felt guilt flame in her chest.

The fact was, she'd give anything to have Pop home.

✳

When she got back to her spot, Pike was there with Vincent and Ronald. They had spread their towels next to the Byrnes'.

Vincent waved. "Hi, Dory."

Dory waved back. "Hi, Vincent. Hi, Ronald."

Ronald looked up from fixing the corners of his towel. "Hi." He pulled a copy of *Amazing Stories* out of his knapsack and sat down next to Pike, who sensed that Ronald was one of his own and struck up a conversation about *Captain America.*

Vincent was still smiling. "Want to go in the water?"

Dory nodded. "Sure." She headed for the deep end and dived in, her skin meeting the icy blue with a glorious shiver. She emerged, swiped her hair out of her eyes, and looked for Vincent. He was at one of the ladders on the side, inching into the water, step by step. Dory's heart warmed inexplicably at the sight of such caution.

She treaded water until Vincent made his way to the middle of the pool, navigating through the bodies oozing a film of suntan oil onto the water's surface. Together, they found a spot where they could touch the bottom.

Evie and Maeve waded past, waving. Both gave Dory and Vincent knowing smiles. What it was they knew, exactly, Dory couldn't say, but she felt her cheeks go pink.

"Evie looks like she's got a stomachache," Vincent observed.

Dory shook her head. "She's just uncomfortable wearing a two-piece."

Near the stairs, a group of women sat on the pool's lip, their ankles dangling into the water. "Is that Miss O'Donnell over there?" Dory asked.

Vincent glanced back. "Yeah. She's here with Miss Ozinskas."

Speaking of uncomfortable, Dory thought. She squinted at the gaggle of ladies. Miss O'Donnell had traded out her wire-rimmed spectacles for a pair of sunglasses. Her hair had been released from the pinched knot she wore at school and could only be described as flowing. And she was reading a particularly steamy-looking issue of *Love Story Magazine*. It was entirely too much for Dory to take in. She ducked under the water to clear her thoughts.

When she surfaced, Vincent cocked his head at her. "She can't make you clap erasers at the pool, you know."

The scent memory of chalk dust rose in Dory's brain, thick and dry. "Yeah."

"You could swim right over and splash her good. There's nothing she could do to you."

Dory smiled.

"You could push her in, even. She has no jurisdiction here."

Dory laughed. She'd never heard the word *jurisdiction* before, but she could tell what Vincent meant. She stood for a long moment, imagining, then shook the image from her mind and grinned. "I'm not a criminal, you know."

Vincent grinned back. "Your landlord would say different."

"That's for sure," Dory agreed.

"Do you know if he ratted on you?"

Dory shrugged. "We haven't heard anything from the city yet, so..."

"Maybe he's forgotten about it."

"Maybe."

"Even so," Vincent said, the groove in his forehead reminding Dory of the groove in Fish's forehead. "You should stay out of his sight."

Dory practically snorted. "Oh, we're definitely staying out of his sight."

For a moment, she considered telling Vincent just *how* out of the landlord's sight they were staying. But there was magic in the secret of the old hotel. Dory felt it in her guts, the magic. And just now she didn't want to share it with anybody.

Vincent kicked off the bottom and floated to a reclining position.

Dory joined him, holding her breath, closing her eyes, and floating on the water's surface. The sun kissed her face, her fingers, the tips of her toes. The rest of her was submerged, carried aloft on six hundred thousand chlorinated gallons. The water filled her ears. It blocked out the noise of the crowded pool, the crowded city beyond.

For a moment, it even seemed to block out the war.

For a moment, the world was right side up.

For a moment, it almost felt like an ordinary summer day.

AWFULLY
HARD
TO BEAR

The last week of June arrived.

Fish started going to the apartment after work each day, sneaking to the mailboxes, eager for Pop's monthly letter.

On Monday, the only envelope in the box was from Captain America.

Fish delivered it that night with a smile.

Pike tore it open, beaming.

Dory rose to look over his shoulder. "What'd you get?"

Pike reached into the thick envelope and slid out a Sentinels of Liberty badge and a membership card.

Fish grinned. "You've gotta sign that, Pike."

Pike got a pencil from room 7 and printed his name on the card with care.

"Now it's official," Dory said. "You've gotta uphold principles and stuff."

Pike pinned the badge on his pajamas. "Billy Donnelly said I can be in his Sentinel club."

"Billy Donnelly's a drip," Dory said, wondering why Pike kept forgetting this.

"When I told him I'd sent in my dime, he said he'd ask the captain about making me a lieutenant."

Fish raised his eyebrows. "Ask the captain?"

Pike nodded. "Billy said he'd write a memorandum about my conduct, to see if Captain America approves."

"Billy Donnelly would be talking about *your* conduct?" Dory was incredulous. "The same Billy Donnelly who practically blinded the phys ed teacher with a pea shooter last year?"

"Yeah," Fish added. "The same Billy Donnelly who got sent home for drawing a picture of Miss O'Donnell on the stairwell wall? *That* Billy Donnelly?"

Pike smiled out one side of his mouth.

"It was actually a pretty good picture," Dory conceded.

✳

On Tuesday, the only envelope in the mailbox was from the New York City Department of Welfare.

Fish trudged into the fifth-floor lobby that night, his face grave.

He put the letter on the card table without a word.

Dory swallowed. "What's it say?"

Fish's voice was pinched. "Read it."

She did. Fulton twined in and out between her feet as the paper trembled in her hands.

Dear Mr. Byrne,

   Pursuant to concerns raised by your landlord, our offices wish to speak to you regarding a matter of child welfare. We have attempted to reach you in person at your residence, to no avail. Therefore, the New York Department of Child Welfare requires that you present yourself to our offices. Should you fail to do so by Friday, July 7, we shall be forced to involve the authorities.

Yours Sincerely,
Edith Martingale
Department Chief

Dory looked up, chewing the side of her thumbnail. "What do they mean, 'involve the authorities'? Aren't *they* the authorities?"

"I guess not," Fish said. "I guess *authorities* means 'police.'"

"Are they gonna arrest us?" Pike asked.

"They can't," Dory whispered. "Nobody knows where we are."

"Are they gonna arrest Pop?" Pike asked.

Nobody knows where he is, either. The thought gnawed a hole in Dory's rib cage. She wanted a letter from Pop so bad, it hurt.

"What are we going to do?" Dory hated that her voice sounded so small.

"I don't know," Fish said. Dory hated that his voice sounded even smaller.

"Maybe you could pretend you're Pop," she whispered.

"I can't," Fish said. "Nobody'd believe I was old enough."

"Maybe if you grew a beard?" Pike suggested.

Fish gave a humorless laugh. "I can't grow a beard."

Dory inspected the still-smooth contours of her brother's jaw. "Not even a mustache?"

"Nope."

"What about a fake one?" Dory offered.

Fish sighed. "Even with a fake mustache, I couldn't pull it off. I'm not like you."

Dory wasn't sure whether she should feel insulted or proud.

But either way, Fish was right. He couldn't pull it off. Just like Dory had been telling him all along, a seventeen-year-old brother and a Pop weren't the same thing.

Not even close.

✳

On Wednesday, the mailbox was empty.

Fish's eyes were red-rimmed when he emerged from the dumbwaiter that night.

"Still no letter?" Pike whispered.

"Not for us." Fish was ashen. "But the Morellos got one."

"What did their pop say?" Dory asked.

Fish cleared his throat. "It wasn't from their pop."

Understanding wormed its way into Dory's head, and she had to look away.

"Who was it from?" Pike asked.

"The Western Union man, Pike," Fish whispered.

Pike bit his lower lip. "Oh."

Dory's eyes burned at the thought of Vincent.

At the thought of Vincent's handkerchiefs, hidden back at the apartment, under her bed.

At the thought of Vincent's kindness.

"What should we do?" she whispered.

Fish shook his head, mute.

Pike sat at the card table. "I think we're supposed to bring them some food."

Dory joined him. "Food?"

Pike nodded. "Millicent Gray said that when her pop got killed, people brought over dinners for weeks."

"I don't know how to make anything good enough to serve to anybody but you two," Fish said.

Pike shrugged. "I think that's okay. Millicent said most of the food they got was horrible. She said she had to eat meatloaf with onions in it three dinners in a row."

"Maybe we should try the delicatessen," Fish said.

✳

They met at Aaronson's late the next day, before dinner at Caputo's.

Mr. Aaronson was behind the counter. He spread his

arms wide as he saw them and smiled a crooked-toothed smile. "Byrnes!" he said. "Come in! Come in! Look at you, Fisher, the man of the house!"

Fish looked at his feet. "Hopefully not for much longer, Mr. Aaronson."

The deli man gave a solemn nod. "God willing. God willing." He turned his attention to Pike. "So tall already, Pike!"

Pike beamed.

"And Doris! Such a beauty! Even prettier than yesterday!"

Fish looked at Dory. "Yesterday?"

Dory faked a coughing fit.

"What brings you in again today, Byrnes?" Mr. Aaronson asked.

Fish shot Dory a look that said he was on to her. "We were hoping we could get something to bring over to the Morellos."

Mr. Aaronson's smile faded. He wiped his hands on his apron. "So sad."

The children nodded.

"So what do you want? Maybe a nice three-meat platter? Pastrami, corned beef, and brisket?"

Fish hesitated. Three meats sounded expensive.

"Maybe some kugel?" Mr. Aaronson asked.

Dory found the combination of noodles and raisins distasteful.

Mr. Aaronson saw her scowl. "Maybe knish? Good for lunch or dinner or in between?"

The children considered this. "That sounds perfect," Fish said.

"How many you want?"

Fish hesitated. "Um...three, I guess? There's three of them."

Dory wondered if he was thinking the same thing she was. *There used to be four.*

"Good, good," Mr. Aaronson said. He retrieved a paper sack from the shelf behind him and reached into the glass case.

Fish dug into his pocket. "How much for the three?"

Mr. Aaronson folded over the neck of the sack. He grinned at them. "No charge."

Fish's mouth fell open. "Oh, we couldn't, Mr. Aaronson. We—"

"'Course you could." Mr. Aaronson swatted away Fish's protests. He looked at Dory. "Your sister here's one of my best customers!"

Dory gave a nervous laugh, keeping her eyes trained on her shoes. She'd figured that if anybody was going to let on about the sheet ladder, it would be Pike, but here was Mr. Aaronson, squealing like a rat.

The deli man handed the sack to a slack-jawed Fish, then noticed Pike at the pickle barrel in the corner. He came from behind the counter with a pair of tongs and lifted the lid. A briny smell filled their noses. Dipping into the barrel, Mr. Aaronson produced a stout specimen, grinned, and handed it to Pike. "You're going to turn into a pickle, you eat so many of these."

Pike took a bite, closed his eyes, and savored it, neatly avoiding Fish's narrow-eyed gaze.

Outside the delicatessen, Dory opened her mouth to explain.

Fish cut her off with a shake of his head. "I don't want to know."

✳

None of them were sure what to say or do when they got to the Morellos' apartment with their offering.

(Nobody knows what to say or do under such circumstances. Being so close to grief is unspeakably difficult. There's a phrase people use sometimes: *bearing witness*. Because witnessing can be awfully hard to bear.)

As it turned out, there wasn't much to it. Neither Vincent nor Irene came to the door. Only an elderly lady Dory didn't recognize but supposed must be Vincent's grandmother.

Fish said how sorry they were. The lady pressed a handkerchief to her nose. Thanked them in a whisper. Took the sack. Set it on a table already piled with food offerings. Closed the door without a sound.

That was all.

It was only as they started down Pearl Street toward Caputo's that Dory realized the lady who looked so old was Mrs. Morello.

✳

On Friday, the last day of the month, the mailbox was still empty.

Empty as Dory's chest felt when Fish climbed out of the dumbwaiter with that no-letter look in his eyes. It was as if her heart had been ripped clean out of her rib cage.

Fish saw the expression on her face. It mirrored his own, but he blinked a few times to clear it. He pulled Pike and Dory to the window seat in the bedroom, and they crammed in beside one another.

"If something happened to him," Fish said, "we would have heard from the War Department."

If something hadn't *happened, we would have heard from him,* Dory thought, but shook the dark notion from her mind. She nodded into Fish's armpit, swallowing an aching need to go see Libby. To see the firm, set strength of her unblinking face and know, just by looking at her, that Pop was fine.

Fulton seemed to sense that his presence was needed, sauntering in from the fifth-floor lobby and leaping onto the Byrnes' laps, where he sprawled and mustered a comforting rumble. He was gaining weight by the day, in inverse proportion to the old hotel's rodent population.

"Letter from Pop or no letter from Pop," Fish said, "we've still gotta pay the rent tomorrow."

"How much is in the mayonnaise jar?" Pike asked.

Fish sighed. "Enough to last us a little while."

Dory scratched behind Fulton's ears. "What's *a little while?*"

Fish shrugged. "This month and next."

"Pop'll write, though." Dory sniffled. "He's just got to."

"He will," Fish agreed. "But still, we need to start economizing."

"What's that mean?" Pike asked.

Fish squeezed them tight. "It means cut back on sandwiches from Aaronson's."

Dory sighed. Economizing didn't sound like any fun at all.

(It sure was a shame they didn't know anything about that diamond, wasn't it?)

✳

Early Saturday morning, they put July's rent money in an envelope and stole cautiously into the apartment building to slip it into Reedy's mailbox. The sound of footsteps in the stairwell sent them fumbling toward the door in a panic, but it was only Mrs. Kopek.

"Gracious, children, you're up early! Where've you been anyway?" She touched Pike on the cheek with a wrinkled hand. "I've knocked on your door half a dozen times this week."

Fish replied in a whisper, "We've been trying to stay out of Mr. Reedy's way."

Mrs. Kopek's eyebrows shot up. "Right. Right." She looked over her shoulder toward the stairwell and lowered her voice. "He was looking for your father, you know. Him and a lady from the city."

Fish nodded. "We know." He squinted at her. "What did you tell them?"

Mrs. Kopek stood a little straighter. "I told them I'd just seen him that very morning, leaving for work."

The children exhaled a collective sigh of relief.

"Thanks, Mrs. Kopek," Fish said. "Really. Thanks a lot."

Mrs. Kopek scowled. "The nerve of him, I tell you." She shook her head. "You just stay clear of him, you hear?"

If she only knew, Dory thought.

"Let me just check my box, and then you come with me to my place," Mrs. Kopek said. "I have something for you."

Dory and Fish exchanged glances, not wanting to stay in the building any longer than necessary, but they followed Mrs. Kopek up the stairs to her apartment anyhow.

She ushered them inside, opened her refrigerator, and pulled out a covered dish, smiling. "Pickled herring and onion rolls."

Dory cringed. *Not even if I were starving to death.*

"You shouldn't have," she said. A little too pointedly.

Fish stepped on her toe. "That's awfully kind of you." He took the dish.

Mrs. Kopek tucked a stray strand of gray back into place. "And something else," she said, her eyes twinkling. "I won two Coney Island combination passes in the auxiliary raffle." She looked down at her feet. "With my bunions, what am I going to do with tickets to Coney Island?"

The Byrnes' eyes lit up. All six of them.

"What *are* you going to do with them?" Dory said.

"Would you like them?"

"Yes!" They shouted in unison. Never had they been more grateful for the bunnies on Mrs. Kopek's feet.

She produced the passes from a drawer and handed them to Pike.

He held one in each hand, beaming. "Gee, thanks, Mrs. Kopek."

"Coney Island's not like it was in my day, of course," she said.

Dory could feel her winding up for a very long story.

"The Steeplechase Park opened in 1897, you know, when I was just a girl."

If Mrs. Kopek was starting in 1897, this could take a while.

Dory cleared her throat. "Thank you so much for the passes, Mrs. Kopek, but we should probably get that herring upstairs and into the refrigerator," she said. "I'd hate for it to go bad."

She sounded remarkably convincing.

✳

Giddy at their extraordinary good fortune, the Byrnes let their guard down and took the stairs to their apartment like regular people.

And there, coming out of the hallway bathroom, was Reedy. He was smoking a cigar.

Smoking a cigar in the bathroom, Dory observed. Which seemed especially vile.

"Morning, kids," he said, releasing a cloud of evil-smelling smoke.

"Mr. Reedy," Fish said.

Pike hid behind his brother.

"It's July."

"Yes, sir," Fish said. "The rent's in your mailbox."

The landlord stuck the cigar in the corner of his mouth. "Mm," he wheezed. "But you know what else July means."

Dory watched as Fish clasped his hands together behind his back to hide the trembling. "I'm not sure we do, sir," he said.

Reedy cleared his throat, more foul smoke billowing. "Your father's got a deadline."

"Yes, sir. He knows." Fish's voice was higher than usual.

Reedy gave a we'll-see-about-that shrug. "It's for your own good, you know. A father who lets his kids run wild's no sort of father." He disappeared into his apartment, leaving only the stench of smoke behind.

Dory forced back tears. She could tell Fish and Pike were doing the same as they let themselves into the apartment and silently stowed Mrs. Kopek's dish in the Frigidaire.

It was only once they'd reached the safety of the fire escape that she choked out a sob. "What are we going to do, Fish?"

Fish swiped at his own eyes. "I swear, Dory, if you ask me that one more time, I'll—"

Snot bubbled in Dory's nose. "But you're supposed to

be the grown-up, Fish! You're supposed to be the one who knows what to do!"

"There's nothing we *can* do, Dory!" Fish shouted. "It's like the letter said. Either Pop shows up at the Child Welfare office by Friday or they call the cops!"

Pike buried his face in his brother's shirttail.

Fish took a shaky breath. Gathered himself. Picked up his brother.

You would have thought Pike weighed about a thousand pounds, for all the effort it seemed to take.

Fish murmured something in his ear that Dory couldn't make out.

The sight of all that tenderness made despair foam in her chest.

Despair that Pop wasn't here to murmur reassurance in all their ears.

Fish, after all, was just seventeen. He only had it in him to carry one of them.

"Look, let's just head back to the hotel, all right?" Fish's voice was broken in places, the shards of it jabbing Dory in the heart.

She nodded. Sniffled. Turned toward the window. "Just a sec." She climbed back inside and collected Pop's favorite shirt, then the photograph of him and Mama in the frame borrowed from Mae, then his service flag, thumbtacks and all.

Still leaking snot, she followed her brothers down the fire escape stairs and past Mr. Kowalczyk's window without a glance at him. He'd certainly overheard the whole sordid episode. Knew they were squirming under Reedy's thumb. She was too tired to care anymore.

She straightened her spine, sucked the tears back in, and gripped Pop's things tight.

If Pop couldn't carry her, she'd carry him instead.

JUST
LEAKING
WONDER

Dory hung Mae's frame on a rusty nail protruding from the plaster just next to the dumbwaiter on the fourth floor. It kept listing to one side, no matter how many times she set it straight, but Pop and Mama didn't seem to mind. Captured forever on the Coney Island sand, they were both happy. They were both alive.

She folded Pop's shirt and laid it in the wardrobe to the right of the door in room 7.

On the second shelf from the top.

(You know. The one with the *diamond*.)

Pop's flag Dory hung in the window, where it ought to have been all along.

She chose the one on the right-hand side in room 7. The one she'd kicked the boards out of the night they arrived at the old hotel. She hung it so that when the breeze filtered in through the rotted planks, it fluttered a little, the way a flag should.

"I'm gonna go outside and see if anybody can see it from below," Dory told Fish. "And then I'm going to walk down to the Battery for a while." She grabbed Pop's binoculars.

Fish didn't object. He sat in the other window seat with Pike, looking awfully tired.

＊

Down on South Street, Dory could only make out the motion of the flag if she squinted hard at the boarded-up window for a good, long time. And the way she figured, there was no reason why anybody would squint hard at a boarded-up window for even a short time, so it wasn't giving them away.

And it was nice. Just knowing the flag was there.

She walked south along the water, its lapping cadence keeping pace with her steps. The bulkhead below the Castle ramparts played the same *hush-hush* rhythm as she climbed the rubble to the top.

Out on her island, Libby stood solid and erect, just like always. Strong. Strong enough to withhold lightning strikes, even. Lightning hit her all the time, in fact. Being the tallest thing around for miles, and being made of metal to boot, she was kind of asking for it.

"The cops are probably coming for us, Libby," Dory said.

A pigeon alighted on a chunk of debris below and looked at her quizzically.

Dory looked over her shoulder, to where she knew the East River eventually led to the prison on Rikers Island, somewhere around where Manhattan met the Bronx. "They'll be sending us up the river." She raised the binoculars for a closer look at the Green Goddess.

"Unless you could work out some sort of a...solution?" Dory said. "Just..." She lowered the binoculars and thought for a long moment. "Maybe Mr. Reedy could get hit by a transit bus or something, like Winston the cat did." She bit her lower lip. "I don't mean that I wish him dead or anything."

(She hadn't wished it. She'd thought about it. But she hadn't wished it.)

"Maybe he could just get amnesia from getting hit by the transit bus."

He'd already given them up to the city, though. So that idea was no good anyhow.

"I'm not asking for a miracle or anything." Dory sighed. "Just, like I said, a solution."

Out in the harbor, Libby stood. Silent. Still. Unblinking.

As if she were really listening.

*

Much as the three of them yearned for a letter from Pop, the Byrnes decided that, given the risk of capture, they ought to limit their mailbox checks. They agreed to go together on Thursday, as soon as Fish got back from the Navy Yard. Safety in numbers and all.

Dory and Pike spent the day hiding out in the library.

She wasn't about to admit it, but Dory had started thinking maybe Pike was onto something, the way he went in for libraries. She'd spent more time in the library in the last month than she had in the whole rest of her life, and it turned out there was some good information to be found there.

On this particular afternoon, for example, the front desk receptionist informed her that *Frankenstein* was a book before it was a movie. And that it was a lady who wrote it.

Who knew?

In any case.

They met Fish as planned, on the corner of Catherine and Monroe. They checked that the coast was clear, then checked again at the door to the building. At the mailboxes, they nodded to one another with looks that said, *This time Pop's letter will be there.*

With Fish posted at the front door and Pike posted at the stairwell, Dory juddered the key into the mailbox and opened the door.

She looked at her brothers and shook her head.

Fish's mouth twitched. "It's only the sixth," he whispered. "Not even a week late."

"Yeah," Pike echoed. "Not even a week." His lip trembled like he might cry, but then he turned abruptly, listening.

He looked back at Dory and Fish. "Someone's coming!"

Dory closed the mailbox with a bang, twisted the key, and pulled to remove it.

It wouldn't come.

Fish's eyes were wide and urgent. "Jiggle it, Dor," he whispered.

She jiggled it. Still, it wouldn't budge.

Pike left his post and ran for the door.

There were definitely footsteps in the stairwell now, and they were coming closer. Dory's hand shook as she wrenched the key this way and that.

"Just leave it, Dor!" Fish said.

Dory was panting. "Maybe if I just—"

"Dory! Leave it!" Fish said.

The key came out of the lock at last.

She held it up, triumphant. "Got it!" As she leaped for the exit, a woman's voice came from the stairwell threshold.

"You must be the Byrne children!"

Dory and Pike were already halfway through the door, but Fish seemed to have frozen on the spot. What on earth could be possessing him, Dory didn't know, but she yanked on his shirtsleeve to try and get him to come to his senses.

"Yes, ma'am," Fish whispered.

Jeez Louise, what's he doing? Dory thought. She yanked harder. Looked at the lady. At her prim suit and heels. Surely, she and her brothers could sprint faster.

"Oh! Lovely, children!" the lady said. "I'm Edith Martingale, from the Department of Child Welfare."

Edith Martingale. The lady from the letter. Her face was lit up with a smile that Dory thought was awfully sinister, coming from a woman who was about to throw the three of them into the orphanage. *Just try it,* she thought, gritting her teeth and trying to figure which of the lady's shins she should kick first.

And here was Fish, shaking the woman's hand.

She was still smiling. "I'm so glad I've run into you, children! I was on my way home from the office, and I thought I'd pop in to let your landlord know how happy I was to get to meet your father today."

To get to meet your . . .

What?

Had they heard right?

They couldn't have.

Did the city lady say she'd met their father?

Met their father . . . today?

For a long moment, the whole world seemed to stop spinning.

Fish looked at Dory, then Pike, his mouth gaping.

Pike started to say something—no doubt, something like *That's impossible!*—but Dory squeezed his shoulder hard.

"Right," she whispered, her brain fogged with the mystery of it. "Pop."

The lady hitched her purse higher on her shoulder. "Anyway, do thank your father for me, children. And I'm sorry to have inconvenienced him. Such a hardworking man."

"Hardworking," Fish murmured.

Dory put a hand on his back to prop him up, afraid

he might pass out. While she was no less baffled than he was, she figured at least one of them needed to pretend to know what was going on.

"Anyway," the lady continued, "I really just came by to set Mr. Reedy's mind at ease." Her eyes crinkled in the corners. "I told him that you children are in excellent hands."

"Excellent hands," Fish repeated.

"I think he was relieved." Mrs. Martingale headed for the door.

Fish held it open for her. "I'm sure he was," he murmured.

They followed her onto Catherine Street, then to the corner of Madison.

Mrs. Martingale turned and faced them. "Well, I'm off, then. And again, I'm terribly sorry about the confusion."

Dory felt a nervous sort of giggle bubbling in her chest, but she stifled it. "Oh, it's no problem at all, ma'am. Thanks ever so much for your concern."

Thanks ever so much? Where had that come from?

"Yeah." Fish sounded winded. "Thank you, Mrs. Martingale." He shook her hand again.

"Good evening, children." Her heels clickety-clacking, the city lady headed north.

Leaving the Byrnes standing there.

Just leaking wonder all over Madison Street.

Fumbling for the explanation that had to be lying around somewhere, Dory looked at her brothers, their mouths similarly agape, then at Mrs. Martingale's retreating form, then at the apartment building.

Her eyes wandered up the side. Past the pharmacy. Past Mrs. Kopek's. To Mr. Kowalczyk's open window on the third floor.

There he was, just like always.

Sitting there at his window, gazing down at them, Mr. Kowalczyk nodded twice.

He gave a very small smile.

Then a very slow salute.

Then he stood, turned, and disappeared into his apartment.

✳

Well, that was a surprise.

Or maybe you're not surprised at all.

Dory, for her part, was entirely surprised. She looked at Pike and Fish, who didn't seem to have noticed Mr. Kowalczyk, and whose brows were therefore still knitted in contemplation of the extraordinary event that had just occurred.

Dory looked up at the third-floor window again. "I'll be back in just a minute."

Bolting up the fire escape stairs and arriving at Mr. Kowalczyk's apartment, Dory called through the open window.

There was no answer.

She called again.

Still nothing.

Mr. Kowalczyk was always at his window. It was the thing that defined him, being at his window. The thing that made him odd and mysterious and a little bit terrifying. Also the thing that apparently allowed him to eavesdrop on the affairs of his neighbors, thereby permitting him to intervene on their behalf. So now, when a person wanted to thank him for it, why on earth would he not be at his window like he was supposed to be?

Fish called out from the street below. "What are you doing, Dor?"

She went to the rail and shouted back. "Just give me a second!"

When she turned around again, Mr. Kowalczyk was there.

"Oh," Dory whispered. "Hi."

He nodded.

Dory cleared her throat. "I guess you saved us?"

He gave the smallest of smiles. "Seems to me you were already doing a pretty good job of saving yourselves. I just gave you a little nudge."

Dory thought about the neighborhood. About all the little nudges it offered.

"Thanks," she said. "I know you don't like leaving your apartment so much, what with you being...you know..."

"A recluse?" he said.

Dory's eyes widened. "Well, yeah." She squinted at him. "This probably took a lot out of you, huh?"

He chuckled. Gave a slow nod. "I fought in the Great War, you know, just like your papa's fighting in this one."

Dory blinked hard against the tears threatening to spill at the mention of Pop.

"So I was glad to help," Mr. Kowalczyk said.

All at once, Dory had an alarming urge to hug Mr. Kowalczyk, but she quickly stifled it because:

1. The window frame would have made it terribly awkward.
2. As you're well aware by now, Dory didn't go in much for hugging.
3. She couldn't be sure, this being really only the second conversation she'd ever had with him, but she had a feeling Mr. Kowalczyk didn't go in much for hugging, either.

"Anyhow," she said, "thanks." There was a sticky glob of feelings at the back of her throat, and she coughed a few times to try to dislodge it. "Thanks a lot."

She decided to just leave it at that.

*

The Byrnes sat at their usual table in Caputo's front window, marveling.

"Mr. Kowalczyk." Fish shook his head in disbelief. "Who would have thought?"

"How do you guess he knew?" Pike asked.

Fish sipped his milk. "Maybe Mrs. Kopek told him."

Dory shook her head. "I think he just listens."

"He must've left his apartment to impersonate Pop," Pike said. "Does that mean he's not a recluse anymore?"

"I suppose so." Fish said.

Pike nibbled an oyster cracker. "It just goes to show you."

"Show you what?" Fish asked.

Pike shrugged. "How people can change."

Dory wondered whether it was Mr. Kowalczyk who had changed, or whether it was the three of them. Maybe they'd just been wrong about him all along, thinking he was odd, when he was really only sad.

Not that there's anything *only* about sadness.

Mr. Caputo appeared with three more glasses of milk and a plate of cannoli.

The Byrnes all sat up a little straighter. Beaming, they thanked Mr. Caputo and dug in, leaving smudges of powdered sugar on their cheeks.

Dory licked cannoli filling from her thumb as a waitress approached from the kitchen. "Mr. Caputo, Angelo's broken another glass and we can't find the dustpan and broom."

"They're in the storage room," Mr. Caputo shouted.

The waitress shook her head. "They're not. I checked."

"Well, check again," Mr. Caputo shouted. "They're always in the storage room, near the canned tomatoes."

Dory closed her eyes. *Not always,* she thought.

She'd used them to dispose of a dead mouse Fulton had brought her on Tuesday evening. Only she never got as far as actually disposing of it. The mouse—and the dustpan and broom—were in room 5, which was already a derelict room and therefore a good place to leave filthy things like dead mice and dustpans.

The waitress looked sheepish. "All right, Mr. Caputo. I'll look again."

Mr. Caputo threw up his hands. *"Dio mio!* I'll look myself." He stomped toward the stairs, muttering something in Italian.

The waitress followed, just to make sure she wasn't going bananas.

Fish stifled a giggle. "He's not going to find the dustpan and broom, is he?"

Dory avoided his gaze, looking pointedly out the window.

"Probably not."

MAKE
IT
COUNT

The Byrnes celebrated their victory over Reedy at Coney Island that weekend.

They hadn't even gotten out of the subway station at Stillwell Avenue before the smell of the place washed over them in a sugary wave, bananas and cotton candy and peanuts and chocolate. A candy store at the station entrance wasn't open for business yet, but the heavenly scent somehow made its way under the door, through the closed windows.

Emerging from the station, the crowd of beachgoers was so thick that, if Dory had simply picked up her feet, she could have been swept along by the tide. Bodies swarmed, moist and sweet in July's humidity. A million people would visit Coney Island that day.

(An actual million. Not just a fancy way of saying *a lot*.)

Fish lifted Pike onto his shoulders as they crossed Surf

Avenue. "You're either up there or holding my hand, okay, Pike?"

Pike nodded, glad to be tethered. "If you get lost, the police put you in a prison under the boardwalk until your folks come to collect you."

"They do not," Dory said.

"They do. Billy Donnelly told me."

"Billy Donnelly's a drip," Fish and Dory said in unison. But the thought of Billy Donnelly in a prison under the boardwalk did bring a grin to Dory's face.

They passed a photo studio where you could get your picture taken as if you were driving cattle on the old-time frontier. They stepped around a puddle of butter dripping from a street vendor's platter of Long Island sweet corn, a nickel a cob. Barkers outside a wax museum promised visions of murder, execution, and electrocution for one thin dime. Dory grabbed Fish's elbow, but he shook his head before she'd even asked. In the distance, they heard the shrieks of riders aboard the Cyclone as it sent them plummeting toward the sea.

At the Steeplechase Park entrance, Pike pulled their tickets out of his pocket and bounced up and down on Fish's shoulders. "Are you going to get a ticket for the rides, Fish?"

Fish smiled. "I'll just watch."

It about broke Dory's heart, the thought of anybody just watching.

She elbowed him. "I'll think of something."

Fish gave her a sideways grin. "Nothing illegal."

The passes were pieces of cardboard with loops of twine for their wrists. Each displayed a carnival barker's cartoon face—its smile equal parts malice and glee—surrounded by a dozen circles for the ride operators to hole-punch as rides were used up. Fish tied the precious passes to Pike's and Dory's wrists until they yelped at the pinching.

The best way into the Pavilion of Fun was through the Barrel of Love, a smooth, revolving tunnel, ten feet wide and sixty feet long. Dory went through at a run. Fish walked on confident sea legs. Pike took the tunnel on hands and knees, which was just embarrassing.

Once they were out, Fish grabbed Pike's hand again and gripped it tight. "Where first?"

Dory and Pike started with the Human Pool Table, a floor of rotating circles that made people collide like billiard balls. Then on to the Spinning Disc, a sort of inverted bowl where visitors clumped together at the peak, only to be thrown to the sides when it began to spin. They rode the El Dorado carousel three times each, Dory hoping to catch the golden ring and win a free ride for Fish. She never did, but her vantage point from the carousel gave her another idea.

She and Pike met Fish at the carousel exit. Pointing to the Steeplechase ride, she poked Fish in the ribs. "That's where we're going to get you your ticket."

The Steeplechase was the attraction that gave the park its name. A sort of mechanical horse race, riders mounted metal steeds and took off on adjoining tracks that dipped and turned, undulating their way around the whole park, inside and out, before reentering the Pavilion and disembarking through The Blow Hole Theater. Which was where Dory now led her brothers.

Dory had heard about the Blow Hole from Rosemary, who had come to Coney Island with her cousins last summer. Rosemary said she'd had nightmares about it for a week after. The theater—really just an exit ramp designed for visitors' entertainment—got its name from the small holes embedded in its flooring. Erratic blasts of wind would blow up the skirts of the ladies exiting the ride. That was bad enough, but it wasn't the source of Rosemary's nightmares.

The nightmares arose because of the clown.

As riders wended their way across the stage, a clown stood waiting to chase them with an electric wand, delivering tiny shocks to anyone he could reach. The clown served the dual purpose of entertaining spectators and ensuring that exiting riders didn't dilly-dally. A sort of maniacal crowd control, if you will.

The Byrnes took spots near the front. Pike's eyes went wide as a lady's skirt was blown up to her elbows.

"Jeepers, Dory," Fish said. "Aren't you glad you wear trousers?"

Dory nodded. "Always."

The clown gave a deranged cackle as exiting riders dodged his prod.

Pike shook his head. "No way am I going on that."

"Me neither," Dory said. Her trousers may have worked for the blow holes, but they did nothing about the clown, who was now shocking a slow-moving gentleman in the hindquarters.

"Can we get cotton candy?" Pike asked.

"Hold on a minute," Dory said. Her plan had to work.

Rider after rider exited, pink-cheeked from the race, the heat, and the anticipation of the gauntlet they now had to run. An older woman held her skirt with one hand and fended off the clown with the other. A soldier used his cap to swat the menace away from his girl.

"Come on," Dory murmured. "It has to happen eventually."

And at last, it did. Three rough-looking boys exited the ride prepared for battle. They taunted the clown with wet raspberries, dodging his prod with ballet-like leaps. One of the boys sidestepped the clown on the front edge of the stage, throwing his arms in the air.

And also his ticket. The combination pass fluttered down toward the crowd, but no one was paying attention to anything other than the chaos on the stage.

No one except Dory. She nudged aside a pair of giggling girls and stepped around a lady with a baby carriage, catching the ticket before it hit the ground. She handed it to Fish with pride.

He looked over his shoulder. "We can't keep this, Dor. We've got to—" He craned his neck, looking for the boy who'd dropped it. He was nowhere to be seen in the teeming crowd.

Dory grinned. "I guess he didn't have a big brother to tie his ticket on tight."

Fish craned his neck again, then looked back at her, a smile creasing his face. He inspected the ticket. Only four holes punched. Eight to go.

He handed it back to Dory and extended his wrist.

They ate packed-from-home peanut butter sandwiches at a picnic table near a stand selling waffles filled with ice cream. Which was a terrible place to eat peanut butter sandwiches. Peanut butter sandwiches do not compare favorably with ice-cream-filled waffles.

(Few things do.)

"Please can we get some?" Pike whined.

Fish succumbed. They ate three perfect waffles, emerging with sticky, satisfied faces.

Fish was wiping Pike's mouth with a paper napkin when a hand tapped his shoulder. The Byrnes turned to find Irene and Vincent Morello standing behind them with waffles.

Irene smiled at Fish. "Hello, you."

He swiped the used napkin over his face to get the whipped cream off his nose. "Hi, Irene!" He stood and seemed to teeter for a long and excruciating moment between shaking her hand and giving her a peck on the cheek, settling at last on a sort of slapdash hug.

Dory peeked out from behind her brother's awkward display and waved at Vincent. He had the look about him that Dory had come to know as the drawn and puckered face of loss.

"Hi, Vincent."

"Hi, Dory."

Fish pulled Pike onto his lap to make room for Irene to sit on one side of him, Vincent on the other next to Dory.

Vincent gave a thin smile. "Thanks for the knishes."

Dory shrugged. "Mr. Aaronson made them." She knew she should tell Vincent she was sorry about his pop, but she also knew she couldn't do it without her nose going all sniffly. She cleared her throat. "So how've you been?" As soon as the words were out, she regretted them. "I mean..." She faltered. *Any numbskull could guess how he's been,* she thought.

"I know what you mean," Vincent said. "I'm all right. Thanks for asking."

For a long moment, neither of them said anything. Dory felt the weight of the burden they'd always shared, Vincent's side now immeasurably heavier.

"I'm real sorry, Vincent."

Vincent rubbed an eye with the heel of his hand. He sighed. "Have you heard anything?"

She shook her head.

Vincent looked away, then back again. "You would have heard if something happened."

"Yeah. But he's never missed a month, writing." Dory rarely wavered in her faith that Pop was okay, but sitting there, so close to the gaping hole of Vincent's bereavement, it was harder to be steadfast.

"You'll hear from him soon," Vincent said. "I'll bet there's a letter waiting for you back at your apartment right now." It was an awfully kind thing to say, especially for a boy who wouldn't be getting any more letters from his pop. He took a bite of waffle, then held it out to Dory. "Want some?"

She shook her head. "If I eat any more and then go on another ride, I'll throw up." She added this to the mental list of things that were nice about Vincent. He was the sort of boy that a girl could talk about throwing up around. "How's your ma?" she asked.

Vincent shrugged. "Sad."

Dumb question, Dory thought. *Again.*

He licked cream from his thumb. "She cooked last night for the first time since Pop..."

Dory thought he was going to say more, but he didn't. She figured it must take a very long time to be able to say the word *died* and mean it.

"She sent us here today," Vincent said. "She thought we needed some fun."

Dory looked around at the glittering, blinking chaos. "A theme park's kind of a weird place to be, huh? What with your pop, and with ours?" The giddy hedonism of the day bumped up against the knot of fear that had been lodged in her stomach since Pop left.

Vincent pulled the maraschino off its stem with his teeth. "Pop always said to make it count."

Everybody's pops had things they always said, Dory supposed.

Make it count seemed like an especially good thing to always say.

She looked over Vincent's shoulder at the carnival games. A throng of soldiers paid a nickel each to throw baseballs at a target: Hitler's face superimposed on the rump of a horse. She reached over Vincent to poke Fish in his side. "Can I have a nickel?"

Fish produced one from his pocket and handed it over

without asking any questions. Coney Island—and Irene—were having a strange effect on him, it seemed.

"Meet us over there," Dory said, indicating the ball toss.

Fish gave the dazed smile of a man in love and nodded at her.

"Come on." Dory beckoned for Vincent to follow.

The uniformed soldiers had finished their turns and were starting to leave, but they paused at the sight of Vincent and Dory, ready to cheer them on. Dory handed her nickel to the carnival man, then nudged Vincent forward.

"That's your nickel, Dory." Vincent's face reddened. "You go."

She shook her head. Looked at him pointedly. "Make it count," she said.

The sides of Vincent's nose bloomed pink. Dory could see the unspeakable agony of his loss, puddling in the corners of his eyes. He took the first ball.

"Give him hell, son!" one of the soldiers shouted.

Dory looked back at him. He was barely older than Fish.

Vincent's mouth went tight. His eyes narrowed at the target's leering grin. He wound up and threw with all his might. The ball connected with Hitler's left eye, the metal target giving a satisfying clunk as cheering and hooting erupted from the soldiers behind them.

"Attaway, boy!" someone shouted.

Vincent turned and looked back at them as a tear slid slowly down the side of his cheek. He glanced at Dory, who gripped her lower lip tight in her teeth and nodded.

"Attaway, Vincent!" she shouted.

He wound up again, hitting his mark straight in the nose this time.

Another cheer rose from the soldiers.

"Easy, boyo," the carnival man said with a smile. "You'll break my target."

That's the idea, Dory thought.

Vincent picked up the third ball and looked at her. He didn't even try to hide the fact that he was crying. Dory held her breath as he reared back and hurled the baseball at Hitler's sneer. The roar of the crowd drowned out the twang of the target as the ball made contact.

Bull's-eye.

The throng of soldiers lifted Vincent onto their shoulders, shouting and cheering and joggling him like a triumphant beach ball. They seemed to feel his fury. Know the reason for it.

When they let him down at last, they offered handshakes and punched his shoulder in congratulations, then dispersed into the seething crowd.

As Vincent approached Dory, she held out a paper napkin, sticky with melted ice cream.

He blew his nose. "Thanks," he said, pocketing the napkin.

Dory thought of the handkerchiefs under her bed. "I owed you one."

✳

The Byrnes and the Morellos stuck together for the rest of the day.

Dory took Pike's hand, leaving Fish's free to hold Irene's.

They rode the Wonder Wheel—the world's largest Ferris wheel, right in their own backyard—as the sun began to sink over Brooklyn's west side. Below them, not a speck of sand was visible on the beach, only bodies crammed together, pulsing with life. Dory looked past the shrieking bathers, toward the endlessness of the blue deep. It was her favorite view, that water.

Vincent's gaze followed hers. He nudged her, pointing east.

"I think I see your pop," he whispered.

Dory blinked at the understanding.

"Yeah," she said. "Me too."

✳

They splurged on Nathan's hot dogs for dinner, sitting at the rail overlooking Surf Avenue. Dory and Vincent shared a malted because:

1. They were economizing
2. They were already full

(They did *not* share a malted because sharing a malted was a romantic thing that a boy and a girl might do if they liked each other. Let's just make that point perfectly clear.)

The five of them crammed onto the subway together for the ride back home, emerging from the Chambers Street station and walking south to their apartments.

Fish never let go of Irene's hand. Dory and Vincent had to look away from the two of them, because it was all just too uncomfortable to watch. Fish may or may not have given Irene a peck on the cheek. Dory was studying a bit of paper bag in the gutter, so she wouldn't have known, except that Pike started giggling.

"Bye, Dory," Vincent said. His cheeks were pink.

Dory crossed her arms over her chest. "Bye, Vincent."

Quick as lightning, while Pike was preoccupied with Fish and Irene, and Fish and Irene were preoccupied with each other, Vincent lurched forward and planted a kiss on Dory's cheek.

It was soft and dry and kind and lovely and altogether surprising in every way.

All the air seemed to leave Dory's lungs at once, and she stood there gaping at Vincent, her knees rubbery.

Vincent looked terrified. "Jeez, Dory," he whispered. "Sorry. I don't know what I was—"

Dory interrupted him. "It's fine."

"Really?" He looked relieved.

She gave a shaky nod. "Yeah."

"Oh. Good."

"I mean," Dory hesitated a moment. "Don't do it again or anything."

"No?" Vincent nodded, his eyes wide. "Okay."

"Not right now, at least."

The others were looking at them.

Dory cleared her throat. "But maybe later," she added.

THE
WHOLE
WORLD

The business with the city settled, the Byrnes no longer had to skulk.

They felt free to come and go from the apartment as they pleased.

They even felt free to lord it over Reedy just a little.

Maybe more than just a little.

Dory dipped into the mayonnaise jar for a present for him. She didn't tell Fish she was doing it, of course, but she did ask him and Pike to come along to deliver it on Sunday evening.

"You got Reedy a present?" Fish asked, incredulous.

"Yep." Dory waggled her eyebrows at him. "A great one."

"I don't want to go see Reedy," Pike said.

"Yeah, Dor," Fish agreed. "Maybe we don't have to

worry about him getting us in trouble with the city any-more, but that doesn't mean I want to start paying social calls. Or exchanging gifts."

"Trust me," Dory said. "It'll be worth it."

Fish looked sideways at her but took Pike's hand and followed her across the hall.

The landlord opened the door, already sneering. "Children."

"Hi, Mr. Reedy," the Byrnes chorused, their smiles a tad too bright.

Reedy's nostrils flared garishly. Dory could see hair bristling out of them. "Don't think you've got me fooled," he said, his breath hissing like the radiators in January. "You pulled the wool over the city's eyes, but I'm wise to you."

"We're not sure what you mean, sir," Dory said, feign-ing innocence. "But we wanted to thank you for looking out for us." She reached into her trouser pocket and pro-duced a fat cigar, handing it over to the landlord with a plastered-on smile. "Here you go."

Fish and Pike looked at her with identical expressions of surprise.

Reedy made a sort of gurgling noise at the unexpected and entirely unjustified gift. A purple vein throbbed in his neck. *Just like Spencer Tracy,* Dory thought, *when he went bonkers and turned into the monster in* Doctor Jekyll and Mr. Hyde.

"Anyhow, thanks," she said, wiggling her fingers in

farewell at the gaping landlord, then pulling her brothers across the hall.

Back in the apartment, Pike's and Fish's brows were still knit.

"Holy mackerel, Dory," Fish said. "You spent money on Reedy? What are you—"

"It only cost a nickel," Dory said. A giggle bubbled in her belly. "I got it on sale at the novelty shop near the bridge."

Pike and Fish looked at her expectantly.

"It's the exploding kind."

✳

Pike and Fish thanked Mr. Kowalczyk. Dory kept telling them they'd need to go to the window to find him, but Fish was stubborn. He said that it just didn't seem proper, thanking a person through a window for a big thing like what Mr. Kowalczyk had done for them. But after they'd knocked on his door on two occasions without success, Fish gave up his principles and followed Dory to the fire escape so he could shake Mr. Kowalczyk's hand.

Pike, who still found the recluse a little bit creepy, gave him a carefully composed note:

Dear Mr. Kowalczyk,

Thank you for impersonating our pop so the three of us don't get sent to the orphanage, which we imagine is pretty terrible. Probably with gruel and spiders and whatnot.

*It was extra swell of you because we know you
don't much like going out and all.*

Your friend,
Pike Byrne

Which Fish said was probably a little bit too honest.

*

Anyhow, it was nice, the not skulking.

Nice, not having to look both ways before coming and going from the apartment.

It was funny, though, how they'd begun to call it that. *The apartment.* Instead of *home.* Home, it seemed, now looked a little like a secret hotel in the Fulton Fish Market.

In the space of only half a summer, their hideout had become a haven.

They'd made the place their own, after all. Pop's things, of course. The portrait with the eyes cut out. The pirate's retreat.

They'd named the rooms, even. That bit was Pike's idea. He'd tacked actual signs to each of the doors:

- MADAM LUNA'S ROOM (Accurate, though not especially imaginative.)
- CHESTER'S ROOM (Again, rather obvious.)
- THE LIBRARY (Pike had started stashing his books there until it was time to return

238

them; Dory thought it was a waste of a
perfectly good room.)

- THE COUNT'S COFFIN (Dory's contribution, for
the room with the cloak in the closet.)
- TREASURE EYE-LAND (Fish was proud of
this one. Though, of course, the *actual*
treasure was upstairs in room 7. You
know. The diamond. In the wardrobe to
the right of the door. Second shelf from
the top. But that's still just between us.)
- THE RAT'S NEST (The derelict room with
the maybe bullet hole in the wardrobe.
Pike had intended to be clever, but the
name was entirely appropriate. The
old hotel's resident rats had indeed
retreated to room 5 with the Byrnes'
arrival back in June, venturing out only
late at night, when Fulton was asleep,
to collect crumbs of pumpernickel
and cruller. Pike ought to have put the
apostrophe at the end, to indicate that
there was more than one rat. Because,
as you know, there is always more than
one rat.)

Above the door to room 7—their bedroom—Pike had
hung a carefully printed sign that read, simply:

THE BYRNES' ROOM

He'd even put the apostrophe in the right place.

∗

But while Mr. Kowalczyk's Pop impersonation had solved the skulking problem, a Pop impersonation wasn't the same as a Pop. As July barreled toward August, the Byrnes' hearts lurched each time they opened the mailbox and found it empty.

They checked Mrs. Kopek's newspaper daily, poring over the reports of the dead and missing, their index fingers coming away black with ink after scanning and then re-scanning the lists, Pop's name blessedly absent.

"If something happened to your father, the War Department would let you know," Mrs. Kopek said.

Everybody said it, in fact. Mr. Caputo. Mr. Aaronson. Mrs. Schmidt.

But with words in the headlines like *besieged*, *smash*, *assault*, *slash*, and *inferno*, it was hard to feel certain. With besieging and such going on, how hard could it be to lose track of a pop or two?

And beyond the soul-crushing worry that something might have happened to Pop, there also lay a very practical concern.

Money.

The lack of it, to be exact.

Fish had begun to make a regular practice of counting out the bills and coins left in the mayonnaise jar, which was still stashed in the linen closet on the fourth floor of the old hotel. It was more coins than bills now, and next month's rent was coming due soon.

"Nobody goes into this jar without asking." Fish looked at Dory, who was hanging upside down from one of the fourth-floor hammocks.

Her scowl was evident, even upside down. "What are you looking at me for?"

"Because I want to make sure you heard me."

She righted herself and dropped to the floor.

"I mean it, Dor. Necessary expenses only."

Dory's nostrils flared. "Why aren't you looking at Pike?"

"Because Pike's eight. I'm pretty sure he's not the one digging into the mayonnaise jar for sandwiches from Aaronson's."

"A few sandwiches aren't going to make that much of a difference." Dory's mouth was tight. "Besides, Pop wouldn't want us to starve to death. Write to him and ask him, if you don't believe me."

"Who said anything about starving to death? And don't bring Pop into this." Fish's voice had gone up an octave or so.

Pike looked up from the domino run he was making. "Are we going to starve to death?"

"No." Fish was resolute. "How did we get from *no more delicatessen runs* to *starving to death*, Doris?"

Dory stamped her foot, knocking over Pike's dominoes and sending Fulton scampering. "I don't know, Fish. You're the grown-up! You oughta know!" She was just being unreasonable now, and she knew it. But she couldn't stop. "Besides, if you hadn't told Pop he could go, nobody'd even be talking about starving to death right now!"

Fish set the mayonnaise jar on the floor with a bang. It reverberated for a long moment as he sat there, like he was deciding whether or not to say something.

At last he did.

"How long are you gonna keep telling me that this is all my fault, Dory?"

Dory only fumed, her blood hot in her neck, her cheeks, her ears.

"Because it isn't my fault. None of this is my fault." A single tear made its way down the side of Fish's nose. "You think I wanted to say *yes* when Pop asked? You think I wouldn't rather have gone myself, if my time had come?"

Dory blinked at him, her heart hammering.

"Because my time would have come in six weeks, Dory. Six weeks from now, I'll be eighteen." He wiped his face on his shirtsleeve. "And I would have been ready. Ready as anybody could be for such a thing. Ready to be the one over there instead of Pop." He paused again. Looked hard at his sister. "So quit saying it's my fault. None of it's my fault. Nobody asked my permission to start this war."

Which was true. All of it.

It was a world war, for heaven's sake. It was in the name and everything.

But it's easier to blame one person than to blame the whole world.

Dory sat herself down, cross-legged, on the weathered

floor of the old hotel and buried her face in her hands, her heart thunking in her ears.

Fish straightened up. "You're right about one thing, though. I'm the grown-up." His voice broke a little, which made it less believable, the grown-up part. "And nobody's starving to death." He sighed. "I started looking for jobs this week."

Dory looked up at him. "You've got a job. At the Navy Yard."

"It's an apprenticeship, remember?" Fish shrugged. "It doesn't pay."

"But it will pay," Dory said. "It'll pay plenty once you're done being an apprentice, I thought."

"Once I'm done," Fish said. "But that's not till next summer. If we don't hear from Pop soon, *once I'm done* won't pay the rent."

"Where are you looking?" Dory whispered, guilt fizzing in her chest.

"I asked Mr. Zuk," Fish said.

Pike cocked his head at his brother. "You want to work at the hardware store?"

Fish closed his eyes for a moment. "This isn't about what I want, Pike. It's about what we need. Mr. Zuk could only take me part-time. So I started asking some of the captains down at the piers. There's a couple of draggers might be looking for crew."

Dory wrinkled her nose at him. "School starts up again soon, though."

Fish waited before answering, as if the words were

hard for him to say. "Plenty of people don't finish high school, Dor." He shrugged. "Pop didn't."

"Yeah, but—" Dory swallowed hard. "You're *going places.*"

"We're all going places, Dor. You and Pike and me. It's just, right now..." Fish sighed. "One of us has gotta go someplace with money."

"If we asked for a dollar from everybody we know," Pike said, "that would be enough to pay the rent, right?"

(If they found the diamond in the wardrobe, that would be enough to pay the rent.)

Dory nodded. "He's right, Fish. I think it's time to start mooching."

Fish massaged his forehead with his fingertips. "No."

"But why not?" Dory pressed. "If it'll keep you from dropping out?"

"Because." Defeat pooled in Fish's eyes. "I told Pop I could manage, and I'm managing."

Pike cocked his head at Fish again. "But Pop always says that the neighborhood—"

"I know what Pop always says," Fish interrupted, his voice unspeakably sad. "And I know the neighborhood would come through if I asked. But asking would feel like I'd failed." He closed his eyes. "And that's not something I want to carry for the rest of my life."

Dory blinked. *The rest of his life.* She looked at the photo of Pop and Mama, hanging there by the dumbwaiter, and thought how sometimes the rest of a life was shorter than anybody wished it to be.

The picture was askew, still, just like everything else in the whole wide world.

And sometimes, when the whole wide world is askew, straightening out one little thing feels like a real victory.

Dory got up with a grunt and righted the picture.

It slipped sidewise again as soon as she let go.

She narrowed her gaze at Mae's obstinate frame. Glanced over her shoulder at Chester's room. Then at her brothers. "I'll be right back."

The envelope was exactly where she'd left it, at the back of room 6's center desk drawer. Mae's letter still nestled against Chester's scrap of poem.

As to me I know of nothing else but miracles

Dory carried the envelope back to the dumbwaiter, removed the framed photograph of Pop and Mama from its nail, and tucked Mae's and Chester's words into the back of the frame's casing.

That extra bit of weight must have made all the difference, for when she replaced it on the nail, the frame hung true.

She silently thanked Chester and Mae. And whoever it was who wrote that poem, even though they weren't so good at rhyming.

The possibility of miracles suddenly felt terribly important.

✳

They paid the rent at the end of the month. But the lumps in their throats were growing more difficult to swallow.

They dealt with those lumps in different ways. As people do.

Pike got teary-eyed and spent a lot more time cuddling Fulton.

Fish got tighter and tighter with what remained of the savings in the mayonnaise jar.

Dory got irritable. She earned herself a good talking-to from Mrs. Schmidt when the bakery lady told her she needed to wash her neck and Dory told her to go jump in the lake. Dory thought she'd said it under her breath, but Mrs. Schmidt apparently had good hearing.

Not even Libby could escape Dory's prickly temper. She sat on the Castle ramparts early one evening as the sun began its descent toward the languid blue of the upper bay, its beams playing on the water, shooting stars of light stretching from Bayonne all the way to Battery Park.

Dory cleared her throat. "Fish told me there are dead bodies down there."

She wasn't appreciating the magic of the sunset, apparently.

"One of the draggers pulled up a skull last winter," she added. "A human one. Like from a shipwreck or a murder or something."

She picked at some loose threads in her trousers, tossed them over the rampart wall and watched them float to the ground like dandelion fur. "And they dumped all sorts of junk in there—old toilets and such—when they tore down some of the apartment buildings in my neighborhood because of the tuberculosis."

Libby was as still as a—well, as a statue, you might say. Clearly Dory was just feeling sorry for herself, talking about dead bodies and old toilets and such. Libby wasn't having any part of it.

"Speaking of tuberculosis," Dory said (which is an unusual way for a person to start a sentence), "you do remember that we've only got Pop left, parent-wise, right?"

She peered through the binoculars, training her eyes on the statue's face. The sun was behind Libby now, its beams setting her sides aglow, casting her face in shadow.

"Don't try that old trick," Dory said. "Look at me when I'm talking to you." She blinked back the tears she could feel gathering. Pulled her legs up to her chest and hugged them. She lowered the binoculars and took a deep breath. Put her chin on her knees. "Sorry," she whispered. "It's just…Fish is gonna quit school…and we haven't heard from Pop…" She swiped furiously at her eyes, afraid that if she let one tear fall, she wouldn't be able to stop the flood. "Anyhow, all I'm saying is…we could kind of use a miracle." She bit her lower lip.

She looked through the binoculars again. Sighed.

"Fine," she said. "Don't answer me."

She rolled onto her stomach, scrambled down the

ramparts without so much as a goodbye, and stomped north along the river.

Dory was too angry to see it, but behind her, the sun was angled in such a way that blinding shafts of light shone through the base of the goddess's torch.

As if it had suddenly been lit.

JUST A
SHINY ROCK,
REALLY

The midsummer heat was punishing. The pavement steamed, the garbage in the alleys ripened, and the metal of the fire escape grate could almost brand you if you sat on it bare-legged.

Always a pleasure, the municipal pool was now a necessity. The Byrnes and the Morellos went together on the first Saturday in August, staking their claim on the spot of shade offered by a scruffy pin oak in the corner of the pool deck.

Pike spotted Billy Donnelly over by the diving boards and took off, speed-walking, so the lifeguards wouldn't blow their whistles at him for running.

Fish and Irene sprawled next to each other, their pinky fingers hooked together on the cotton terry border where their towels met. Dory couldn't help but smile, seeing Fish there like a regular big brother doing a regular thing like holding hands with his girlfriend. Things having been so very unregular lately.

Vincent was smiling at the scene, too, like perhaps he understood about things being unregular.

Dory thought maybe the peck on the cheek after Coney Island might make things uncomfortable with Vincent. She'd pictured it like a fence between them. A giant, electrical, kissing fence. So it was nice, the way things actually felt. Entirely natural.

"Wanna go in the water?" she asked.

"Sure."

Dory headed for the deep end, surprised to find that Vincent followed along behind, rather than inching in at the stairs. They passed Miss Ozinskas, sitting in a lounge chair near the wall, and Miss O'Donnell, perched on the pool's lip, her feet in the water.

Vincent nudged Dory, then pointed at a spot a yard or so beyond the assistant principal. He raised his eyebrows conspiratorially. "That looks like a good place to jump in."

Dory glanced from the spot to Miss O'Donnell, then back again, gauging the potential splash radius.

Which . . . well.

She looked at Vincent. "Cannonball?"

He nodded. "Yeah."

Dory grabbed his hand and squeezed it tight.

"Make it count," she said.

✳

Late the following week, Fish was offered a spot on the crew of a dragger called the *Oonagh*. He could start at the end of the month after finishing out the summer at the Navy Yard, the captain said. He could even get a small advance on his paycheck to cover September's rent.

Which ought to have felt like a victory.

And it did.

Except that it didn't.

The Byrnes sat in their room at the old hotel that Saturday evening, dipping yesterday's caraway rolls from Schmidt's into bowls of tomato soup. Even tomato soup— widely known as the most comforting soup there is— couldn't dispel the sense of gloom.

Dory lay on her stomach by the open window. A storm had come through that morning, bringing blessed relief from the feverish heat. A breeze grazed her shoulders as she tried to craft a V-Mail to Pop.

She hadn't gotten very far. It was hard, figuring what to say. Back when Pop's letter was only *a little late*, she was able to write things like *Sure you're real busy over there!* and *Can't wait to hear from you!* and then yammer on about dumb stuff like Mrs. Kopek's feud with the Doyle sisters, or a joke Abbott and Costello told on the radio.

It was easy to *make it cheerful* then.

But by now, weeks had passed, and every time Dory sat down to write, she couldn't think of a thing to say beyond *It's August, Pop,* and *Where are you?* and *We're all so scared.*

Fulton—who had a sixth sense about where and when his services were needed—ambled in from the fifth-floor lobby, kneaded his paws on her rib cage, settled himself against her side, and fired up the purring. Dory dipped her finger in her soup bowl and let him lick it.

Fish slouched in one of the ghost chairs, his head against the faded paisley of the wingback, his eyes closed.

Pike sat in a window seat with July's *Captain America*. Before the news about the *Oonagh*, Fish said they couldn't spare the dime for the August issue.

"When you get paid," Pike said, "then can I get this month's issue?"

"Sure," Fish said.

"We're gonna need new school supplies soon, too," Pike added.

"Mm-hmm," Fish murmured.

"The zipper on my pencil case is busted," Pike said.

"Okay."

"And I need new shoes." Pike held up a foot. "These have holes."

"All right," Fish said.

"Me too?" Dory asked.

"Uh-huh."

Dory narrowed her gaze at Fish. What had happened to him? Why wasn't he telling Pike to use a safety pin if the zipper was busted? Why wasn't he telling them they ought to look through the hand-me-down shoes in the hall closet back at the apartment and find some that fit?

It was unsettling, him saying *yes* to everything.

She picked a caraway seed from between her teeth. "Hey, Fish?"

"Yeah?"

She mustered confidence from somewhere. "Pop's going to come home, you know."

Fish gave a tiny nod. "Sure. He is."

"And when he does," Dory said, "everything can go back to the way it's supposed to be."

"Mm-hmm."

Dory's heart pinched at the sight of her brother, sitting there in the ghost chair, looking like he was being crushed by something. She'd heard the expression *the weight of the world on his shoulders* before, but she'd never really seen it for herself until now.

From the looks of it, the world sure did weigh a whole lot.

"Hey, Fish?" she said again.

"What?"

"Until he does come back..." She swallowed. "You're doing a real good job."

She thought of all the times she'd told him otherwise, and felt a little sick to her stomach.

Fish's nose went pink at the sides. "Thanks."

"I mean it," Dory said. "You going to work on a dragger for us? Giving up school for us? That's the kind of stuff real grown-ups do."

Fish gave the saddest smile anybody's ever seen. "Who knew that's what it meant, being a grown-up?"

"Hm," Dory murmured. Leaving the remains of her

soup to Fulton, she got up and crossed to where Fish sat, squashing herself in beside him, her bony hip smashed against his bony hip in a way that wasn't at all comfortable.

Except that it was.

They sat there, piled into the ghost chair, for a long time. Listening to Pike turn the pages of *Captain America*. Looking out the window where, in the space between the boards, they could see the night sky, as star-filled and perfect as any sky had ever been.

Dory poked him in the ribs with her index finger. "I'm real sorry, Fish."

He threw his head back and looked at the ceiling. "Aw, jeez, Dory, what'd you do this time?"

Dory shook her head. "I didn't do anything." She cleared her throat. "Recently." She laid her ear on his shoulder. "I only meant I'm sorry for blaming you."

"Oh," Fish said. He laid his head on top of hers. "That's all right."

Dory supposed that was another rotten part of being a grown-up. Taking the rap for stuff you'd had nothing to do with.

"But still," she said. "I'm real sorry."

"It's okay, Dor." He planted a kiss in her hair.

She breathed in the scent of her brother. Of oil and sweat and the sea, his shirt still ripe from his week at the Yard.

Which gave her an idea.

She nudged him in the side and hoisted herself out of the chair. Turned to face him, her gaze direct and purposeful. "There's something you oughta have," she said.

"What?"

"Pop's shirt."

Fish squinted at her. "Which one?"

"His favorite," Dory said.

Her favorite, more importantly.

"I can't take Pop's shirt," Fish said. "He'll want it. When he comes back."

"Then return it to him." Dory shrugged. "But for now, at least..." She gathered herself to say the words she hadn't been able to say since November. "You're the pop." She gave a nod to emphasize it. "And you're a real good one."

Fish looked like maybe the world was a couple of pounds lighter.

Dory smiled at him, took a deep breath, and went to the wardrobe.

(You know the one.)

She opened the heavy wooden door and reached for Pop's shirt, neatly folded on the second shelf from the top.

(Yep. That shelf.)

She grabbed the shirt and swept it out with a flourish.

So much of a flourish that the flap on the left-side pocket caught the diamond earring on its edge and sent it skittering.

To the other side of the shelf.

It made a skittering sound, even.

But it turns out that the sound a diamond earring

makes as it skitters from the left side of a wardrobe shelf to the right side of a wardrobe shelf isn't all that different from the sound a shirt button makes when that shirt is swept out of a wardrobe with a flourish.

Pike, engrossed in a scene where Captain America battled Nazis and Gargoyles simultaneously, didn't notice.

Fish, his heart thrumming in his ears at the tenderness of his sister's gift, didn't notice.

And Dory?

She didn't notice, either.

Dory Byrne, who'd been walking around with a sort of a sour taste in her mouth for months and months now, suddenly tasted nothing but sweet as she crossed back to the ghost chairs, held Pop's shirt up to let Fish slip into it, and fell into her brother's arms so he could hold her tight. He was scrawnier than Pop. And he smelled different. But if she closed her eyes and held her breath, she almost couldn't tell the difference between the two of them. Love-wise, they were indistinguishable.

It was a very long while before either one of them let go.

And all that very long while, the diamond—just a shiny rock, really, if you think about it—sat right where it had sat for more than half a century.

On the second shelf from the top.

In the wardrobe to the right of the door.

In room 7 of the old hotel.

The treasure—well, *that* treasure—remained buried.

For now, at least.

AND YET

You were probably thinking the diamond was the big miracle, weren't you?

Well. That's all right.

It's kind of a dirty trick, after all, letting you know there's a diamond in the wardrobe and then just leaving it there, a shiny rock instead of a miracle.

Sorry.

But not that sorry.

If we're being honest here.

*

A sort of a yawping sound woke Dory early the next morning. It was insistent, the yawp. It demanded attention. She put her pillow over her head and tried to block it out, but the yawp simply would not be ignored.

Dory unwound herself from her sheets, dislodging a

disgruntled Fulton from the foot of her bed. He glared at her, shook himself, and leaped to the floor of room 7, then to Pike's bed, his tail twitching with indignation.

There it was again, the yawp. It was coming from outside.

Dory looked at Fish and at Pike, both still sleeping soundly, oblivious to the ruckus. Climbing into the window seat and gentling aside Pop's service flag, Dory stuck her head through the window's remaining planks. Down below, the fish market was Sunday-silent, its stalls shuttered for the weekend.

The bellowing sounded again, deep and rumbling. It came from the harbor. Dory couldn't see from her vantage point, but it must be a foghorn, she figured. A ship making its way past Libby. Ships did that sometimes, the yawps their way of tipping their hats to the great lady.

Dory's stomach groaned. There was one stale cruller left in the bag on the card table out in the fifth-floor lobby. She looked at Pike and Fish again. Considered devouring it, herself, before they woke. But the sweet taste in her mouth from last night still lingered, and she decided to content herself with just her fair share of the pastry.

She'd only made it a few steps, though, before the caterwauling from the harbor stopped her in her tracks. She stood there for a long moment, suddenly aware that her heart was plunking harder than usual. A little faster, maybe. Not like she'd just run up a flight of stairs or anything. Not like she'd just watched a scary scene in a picture. No.

But the ship's bellowing was stirring something in her. In her guts, somewhere.

Pop's binoculars hung from the room 7 doorknob. Dory grabbed them, returned to the window seat, and stuck her head through the planks again. Adjusted the viewfinder and squinted out toward where the river's mouth opened into the harbor.

From her vantage point in the window of the old hotel, she saw nothing of note.

And yet.

Her heart.

She crossed to Fish's bed and squeezed his shoulder. "Fish," she said. "Wake up."

He murmured a couple of nonsensical words, like he was in the tail end of a dream, then opened his eyes and squinted at Dory. "What is it, Dor?" His voice was filmed with sleep.

"There's something going on downstairs."

Fish sat up. "In the restaurant?"

"No." Dory shook her head. "In the harbor."

"What?" Fish looked alarmed. "What's happening in the harbor?"

"I..." Dory paused. "I don't know, exactly."

But she did. She did know, somehow.

Pike rolled to his stomach, his arm flopping over the side of the bed. Fulton, who had had just about enough of all this early-morning bustle, got up with a huff and retreated to the fifth-floor lobby for some peace and quiet.

"Pike!" Dory said. "Wake up."

The foghorn sounded again. Closer now.

Fish threw back his bedsheets and climbed into the

window seat. "Is that what you're talking about? That ship's whistle?"

"Uh-huh." Dory handed him the binoculars.

He trained them toward the harbor. "There's something there for sure," he said. "But I can't make it out yet."

Dory picked up yesterday's clothes from the floor and joined Fulton in the lobby to change in relative privacy. "Get dressed!" she shouted. "Both of you!"

Pike sat up with a grunt. "Why?"

Fish was already pulling on Pop's shirt. He nodded pointedly at his sister as she returned. "Because Dory says so."

*

Emerging from the alley and rounding the corner onto South Street, Dory took the binoculars from Fish and looked toward the harbor. There, steaming past Governor's Island and headed straight for them, was the source of the yawping.

She focused the lenses. Peered out at the hulking ship. At the insignia on her funnel.

A red cross.

Dory gasped. She lowered the binoculars. Looked at her brothers.

"It's a hospital ship."

Fish and Pike stood there, slack-jawed, for a long moment.

Fish was breathless. "And you think…" He trailed off.

Dory only nodded at him.

Pop was on that ship. He had to be.

Because…her heart.

The three of them turned in unison and looked south. Fifty or sixty yards on, they could see uniformed men and women unfolding camp beds on the brick-lined wharf. A small field of stretchers with legs.

They headed along the waterline, keeping their eyes on the ship's funnel. The vessel had passed beyond White-hall now and was making its way up the river.

Fish wiped sweat from his brow as they arrived at the makeshift hospital.

Dory looked at the stretchers. "How many beds do you figure there are?"

"Seventy-two," Pike said.

Dory squinted at him. "Seventy-two, exactly? How'd you figure that out?"

Pike shrugged. "Six rows. Twelve beds to a row. Six times twelve."

Dory took his word for it. She'd never bothered to learn her times tables as far as twelve.

Ten minutes, and the ship was sidling up to the pier, grunting and heaving. The river of smoke pouring from her funnel became a stream. Then a creek. Then trickled away entirely.

Dory used the binoculars to scan the faces on deck. But it was disorienting, looking through the glass. She lowered them and slid one arm through the strap, letting them dangle against her side.

Meanwhile, a crowd was gathering in the street.

Some of them just looked curious. A nun heading

south toward Our Lady of the Rosary. A boy about Pike's age, chasing a dog.

Some looked anxious. A young woman holding a small girl's hand. An older woman and an even older man, his arm around her shoulders. A middle-aged man in uniform, his arm in a sling. With his free hand, he removed his cap as if anticipating the need for reverence. They all stood on tiptoe, craning their necks this way and that, like they were expecting someone.

Dory approached the man in the sling. "Excuse me?"

He turned to look at her. "Yes?"

"Do you know somebody on that ship?"

His eyes crinkled in a smile. "My brother."

"He was wounded?"

"In France."

Dory gulped. "So that ship's coming from France?"

"Well, there and other places. Men wounded in the European theater."

"Is your brother okay?"

"Yeah. Not going to be doing any more fighting, but he's okay."

Dory bit her lip. "That's good." She glanced at the ship, then back at the uniformed man. "How d'you know he's on there? Your brother?"

Again, the man smiled. "Our ma got a telegram."

Dory nodded. "Thanks, mister."

She returned to Pike and Fish and repeated what she'd learned.

"We didn't get a telegram," Fish said.

Dory looked at him, needing him to keep on believing. Like believing hard enough could make it real.

On the ship's deck, uniformed men and women bustled about. Some stood, waving. Some pushed wheelchairs. Some were pushed in them. Some went about the business of securing the ship and readying her to make port.

This takes a long time. A very long time. It feels long when you're a passenger on a ship, anxious for solid ground beneath your feet after a long while on the tilting sea. It feels long when you're waiting for such a passenger to return from, say, a fishing expedition or an island cruise.

For the Byrnes, it was an eternity.

The first passengers disembarked after about a half an hour. Some were wheeled down the gangway on rolling stretchers. Some were pushed in wheelchairs and transferred to the camp beds waiting on the wharf. Some were bandaged. Most weren't. Some had their eyes closed as if they were asleep. Most didn't. Pike and Dory and Fish watched as some of the men were wheeled toward whatever transport would take them the rest of the way home to the cities where they lived. Poughkeepsie. Scranton. Dover.

Dory ached to stop them as they went by. To ask them about Pop. But she didn't.

A stream of men began descending the gangway of their own accord, their injuries starkly labeled in plaster and gauze. The Byrnes silently evaluated each face, hoping they might catch Pop's lopsided grin, the cleft in his chin that Dory always said looked like the coin slot in a pinball machine, back before the mayor dumped all the pinball machines in the river because he counted them as gambling.

They wondered if they would recognize his bouncing gait. If he was still able to bounce.

If he was on the ship at all.

"How many do you reckon have got off so far?" Dory asked.

"Fifty-seven," Pike said.

"Are you counting?"

"Yeah." Pike pulled on Fish's shirt, a wordless request to be lifted for a better view. Fish obeyed, hoisting his brother onto his shoulders.

A man on deck leaned so far over the rail he looked as if he might tip. He scanned the crowd until he found the old couple, then waved furiously. The woman pulled a handkerchief from her purse and waved it as the soldier headed toward the ramp that would bring him home.

"Seventy-one, seventy-two," Pike said.

The line of soldiers felt endless.

A sea of men who all somehow managed to not be Pop.

Dory felt her throat tighten with every uniform that passed. Her heart was walloping her ribs so hard, she was sure Pike and Fish could hear it.

The man with the sling was gone. His brother must have disembarked already. The older couple was just now reuniting with their son, which made the Byrnes take a few steps back. They told themselves it was for a better view, but the truth was that it was just too hard to be near a jubilant reunion that wasn't their own.

"That's a hundred and twenty," Pike whispered.

"Cut it out, Pike," Dory said. "You're only going to drive us all crazy with the counting."

Pike sniffled. "Sorry." His lips kept up their silent tally.

Fish squeezed Pike's knee with one hand and wrapped his other arm around Dory. "Even if he's not on this ship," he said, "it's okay." He held Dory tight. "It's going to be fine."

Dory shrugged him off. She could feel him starting to lose hope, and losing hope was not something she could bear.

The next man was too tall to be Pop. The one after that was too short.

Next came a man with a bandage around his head, gripping the rail tight as he made his way down the ramp. His gait had no bounce to it the way Pop's did.

War tends to do that to people—it takes away their bounce.

And the man was too far away, still, for the children to see the cleft in his chin.

He stepped onto South Street, moved out of the line of men, and dropped to one knee.

Dory figured that the man couldn't walk anymore. That his injured legs had given out before he'd taken even two steps on American ground.

That wasn't what had happened. The man could walk just fine. He'd only knelt to touch the bricks of the East River waterfront. To feel their familiar grit in his hand. To offer thanks that he was home.

When the man stood up from his prayer, he locked eyes with Dory.

And Dory Byrne would know Pop's eyes at any distance.

She took off, sprinting, her feet hardly touching the ground, her legs pumping like they'd never pumped before. Pop dropped his duffel bag and lunged forward and in a matter of moments, Dory had launched herself into the air, flinging herself at Pop, whose strong arms were ready for her. He grabbed her and spun her, one arm pinning her to his chest, the other tangled in her hair, pulling her face to meet his, planting scratchy kisses behind her ear.

Fish and Pike had made it, too, now, and Pop extracted his hand from Dory's hair and grabbed Pike, hoisting him on one hip and clinging to him like a drowning man would a life raft.

Fish stood there for a few seconds, tears sliding off the sides of his nose and into his mouth, his grin so wide it looked as if his face might crack. Pop put Dory and Pike down and wrapped both arms around his oldest boy, who wasn't a boy at all anymore.

The Byrnes—all of the Byrnes now—stood there on South Street for practically forever, hugging one another in turns, murmuring words that weren't decipherable. Words like *missed* and *scared* and *love* and *proud* and *never, never, never again.*

Words that don't need to be heard clearly in order to be understood just fine.

Pop told them what had happened to him. That there was a scar underneath his bandage about six inches long. He told them why there'd been no letters. No telegram.

Something about the invasion and something about an enemy hospital.

They could hear all the details eventually. The details didn't matter yet.

All that mattered was Pop being there.

Fish grabbed Pop's duffel.

Pop lifted Pike onto his shoulders, gingering him around the bandage, then threw one arm around Dory, the other around Fish. "Let's go home," he said.

Behind Pop's back, Dory grabbed Fish's arm, and he grabbed hers.

They started for home, a knot of family that wouldn't be untied again.

A couple of blocks ahead, Caputo's rolled-up awning was visible in the noonday light. Fish gave Dory's arm a squeeze, then raised his eyebrows at her, flashing a meaningful grin.

The grin's meaning was: *We've got some explaining to do.*

And also: *We've gotta go get the cat.*

Dory gave him a twitch of a nod.

She longed to take Pop around back to the alley and let the old hotel speak for itself. But he'd just survived storming a beach and getting captured by Nazis and heaven only knew how much else the war had thrown at him. Dragging him through Caputo's kitchen window and hauling him up three flights in the dumbwaiter just might finish him off.

Their feet slowed near the door to the restaurant. Pop peered through the darkened windows. "Mr. Caputo's taken good care of you, I bet?"

"Very good care of us." Pike rested his chin on Pop's head.

Fish looked up at his brother and winked. Put his finger to his lips.

"So has the rest of the neighborhood," Pike added.

"Just like I said." Pop smiled.

Dory squeezed Fish's arm. She cleared her throat. "And so has Fish." She beamed at her brother. "Just like you said."

Fish beamed back at her. It was a whole lot of beaming.

Pop mashed their faces into his chest in a fierce embrace. "I'm so proud of you three."

"We're proud of you, too, Pop," Dory murmured into the blue of his shirt. When he released them, her eyes made their way past Caputo's awning, up the façade of the old hotel.

She exchanged another glance, another nod, with Fish.

"Look up there, Pop." She pointed.

He did, shielding his eyes with his hand.

"Top floor. The window on the left." Dory cleared her throat. "It's your service flag."

If they squinted, they could just make out the flag's edge. Its red border and gold fringe.

Pop squinted harder. "Huh?"

"Your service flag," Fish whispered. "It's up there."

Pop looked back at them, a bewildered smile on his face. "How the heck did it get up there? I thought those floors were abandoned."

"They were." Pike grinned down at Fish and Dory. "But they're not anymore."

The bandage around Pop's head puckered as he knit

his brow in good-natured confusion. "Well," he said, "it sounds like there's a story to tell here."

Fish raised an eyebrow at Dory. "More than one."

Pop looked at the boarded windows again. "So what's up there, exactly?"

Dory turned to face her family. All of it.

And though she hadn't found the diamond (hadn't found it yet, that is...nobody's saying it couldn't happen someday), she answered Pop with confidence.

With a single word.

"Treasure."

She saw it everywhere, now.

Seafood stew.

A Zippo lighter.

Stale crullers.

Snotty handkerchiefs.

Pickled herring and onion rolls.

A crummy old hotel.

A whole neighborhood, full to bursting with treasure. Throwing it in your face every chance it got. Even— maybe especially—when you weren't looking for it.

Dory looked at Pop. He hadn't been home an hour yet, so she couldn't believe what she was about to say. But there was something she had to do.

"Can you wait here for me for just a sec?"

Pop cocked his head at her. "Where are you going, honey?"

"I'll only be ten minutes," she said. "That's all I need. And it's important."

Fish looked at her knowingly. "Sure, Dor." He nudged Pop. "Let her go. If Dory says it's important, it's important."

Dory grinned at her brother.

And took off at a sprint for the Castle.

∗

Out on Bedloe's Island, Libby stood there, motionless.

Only, she wasn't, really. Motionless, that is. The Eiffel Tower man who'd built her skeleton made sure she'd sway a bit in a storm. Swaying in a storm is important, it turns out. If you don't give a little, you'll break.

Dory trained the binoculars on the statue.

She was still panting from her half-mile run. Her heart, its missing chunk back in place now, hammered joyfully.

Sunlight reflected off the ripples in the harbor, playing on the folds of the statue's gown. If you squinted at her, the trick of the light almost made it look like she was dancing.

"Thanks, Libby." Dory paused. Gathered herself. "For everything."

She peered out at the goddess's face.

At her stone gaze, enigmatic and motionless.

Even years and years later, Dory Byrne would swear to anybody who'd listen that she saw her smile.

AUTHOR'S NOTE

*Sloppy Louie's, the real-life Caputo's, was a fixture in New York's
Fulton Fish Market neighborhood from 1930 until 1998.*

The Byrnes' old hotel is there for you to see. You'll find it
right where it's been since the middle of the nineteenth
century, on the very southern tip of Manhattan, in what
used to be the Fulton Fish Market and is now part of the
South Street Seaport Museum.

I learned of the old hotel in a 1952 *New Yorker* essay
by the late, great Joseph Mitchell. Mr. Mitchell chronicled
New York like no one else. His essays are a treasure chest.
He also—along with Louis Morino, owner of Sloppy
Louie's Restaurant, a fish market staple from 1930 until

1998—braved the actual, ancient, unused dumbwaiter that was the only way to get to the building's upper floors. Mr. Mitchell and Mr. Morino really did find the remains of the old Fulton Ferry Hotel up there: bedsteads, bottles, ledgers, and what the museum's historian has referred to as "honorable debris." I owe a very great debt of gratitude to Joseph Mitchell for letting me dream up the rest of it.

The Statue of Liberty really did go dim during World War II. Only the tip of her torch and a few bulbs around her base were lit, to keep boats from slamming into her. And she really did blink on D-Day in 1944. Had Dory known Morse code, she may have realized that the Green Goddess was flashing *V* for victory.

The poem fragment Dory finds in Chester's room is from Walt Whitman. I like to think that maybe when Dory grew up, she sought out the rest of it. Even though Uncle Walt didn't bother to make it rhyme.

The snippets of media mentioned are all real. The "aggression and barbarism and wholesale murder" speech Pop references when he's considering whether or not to go off and fight was FDR's Fireside Chat of September 8, 1943. The "eyes of the world are upon you" speech that the children overhear on the evening of the D-Day invasions was Eisenhower's address to his troops, replayed on American networks that evening. And the prayer Dory walks in on after receiving Libby's Morse code message was Roosevelt's D-Day prayer, broadcast live that night. Likewise, the newsreel Dory and Pike watch while *not* stealing from Bing Crosby is based on a real one that references a soldier bringing home a Nazi flag to use as a doormat.

I feel tremendous respect and gratitude for those who served and sacrificed—both abroad and on the home front—during World War II, so I hope I'll be forgiven for the historical liberties I took in the name of story. For example, while it wouldn't have been out of the question for soldiers to send money home as Pop did, most would have had paycheck deductions set up through stateside banks. But paycheck deductions didn't feel like the stuff of storytelling. In terms of the timing of events: New York City public schools would likely have let out later in June than the Byrnes' fictional PS 42 did, but with Libby's message coming through on D-Day, I wanted Dory and family to be free to seek refuge in the old hotel sooner. The same goes for the timing of Pop's homecoming. In reality, wounded soldiers would likely have been treated on hospital ships near the conflict zone, and their wait for transport home after D-Day would have been considerably longer. When they finally made it, ships probably wouldn't have docked in the East River. But it was irresistible, having Pop return when, where, and how he did. And while shipbuilding apprenticeships at the Brooklyn Navy Yard were very real, my understanding is that such things were typically after-high-school alternatives to college, as opposed to the sort of summer arrangement I made up for Fish. Lastly, thoughtful early readers noted that, while much of the story is set in summertime, there is no mention of the Independence Day holiday. From the historical accounts I could find, Fourth of July celebrations were quite muted throughout the war, so the Byrnes may well have gone several years without much marking of the holiday. President Roosevelt was even quoted as saying that the day ought to be celebrated "not in the fireworks of make-believe, but in the death-dealing reality of tanks and planes and guns and ships." The omission is therefore intentional, but I thought it was important to note it as such, here.

Dory's world is very much the world of my father and grandmother. I grew up on their stories of old New York, and I so wish my grandmother were still around to recognize them in these pages. Jocko the gorilla, for example, was real, and really did throw things at spectators, though it was at the Staten Island Zoo, not the one in Central Park. Also real were Professor Heckler and his flea circus. You can even find a video of their appearance on Lenny Bruce's show in the 1950s, though they'd been performing at the dime museum on Forty-Second Street for decades by then. And Coney Island. The Spinning Disk, the Wonder Wheel, and the Steeplechase. During the war, one of the carnival games really did invite visitors to take aim at Hitler's face, planted squarely on the rump of a horse. The clown with the electrical wand was also real, though my dad didn't recall that particular horror until I read about it in a book and asked him if he'd ever run the gauntlet of the Blow Hole Theater. He had.

Sometimes, the best stories aren't the made-up ones.

ACKNOWLEDGMENTS

The fact that I get a second chance at an acknowledgments section still feels like a dream. All the gratitude I felt with the first has grown tenfold since, as my heart is full with the understanding of just how much care goes into the birthing of a book. What a gift it is to sit here worrying that I'll leave somebody out of these final pages. So many people to thank and to love.

My warmest thanks to every young (and less young!) reader who takes the time to reach out with kind words. It means more to me than you will ever know. And to all the big-hearted booksellers, librarians, and teachers who work so tirelessly to support writers and get books to kids. Your generosity has been on my heart throughout the writing of this book. Thank you.

I spent a magical hour in what remains of the Byrnes' old hotel in August 2021, thanks to Martina Caruso, director of collections, and Michelle Kennedy, collections and curatorial assistant, at the South Street Seaport Museum. The museum was closed at the time due to the pandemic, so their willingness to put on masks and give me a tour of this extraordinary and lovingly preserved space was beyond gracious. It was an experience I will never forget.

Thank you to Dr. Stephanie Hinnershitz at the National World War II Museum in New Orleans. She kindly answered my questions about correspondence between soldiers and their families, and about wounded soldiers' return home after D-Day. The historical liberties taken around those topics are my own, and I thank Dr. Hinnershitz for her understanding.

Kathryn Green, wisest and kindest of literary agents! Thank you for sharing this road with me. For celebratory lunches and drinks. For answering questions with honesty and thoughtfulness. For your generous spirit and wise counsel. I couldn't ask for a better partner in this endeavor.

I remain so very lucky to be part of the Holiday House family. The publishing ride is a wild one, and I have felt nothing but supported by you all. Thanks to the managing editor Raina Putter, the rights director Miriam Miller, and the endlessly lovely marketing team: Terry Borzumato-Greenberg, Michelle Montague, Alison Tarnofsky, Bree Martinez, and especially Sara DiSalvo, who only ever responds to the questions of this clueless author with kindness. Gratitude to copy editor Janet Renard, whose extraordinary fund of knowledge and keen attention to detail are so very much appreciated. And to Doni, who may be retired, but whose above-and-beyond generosity will never be forgotten.

Gilbert Ford: Thank you for bringing Dory and her New York to life so brilliantly in the cover art.

Most of all, to Margaret Ferguson: I will never have words enough to clearly express what a joy it is to work with you. Thank you, from the bottom of my heart, for thinking about the crafting of a children's novel at a level that I can only aspire to, and for communicating your wisdom with such gentle eloquence. I am profoundly grateful to be in your hands.

I had no idea, when I started down this publishing road, that I would get friends out of the deal. What an unexpected blessing. Summer and Jill have been my beloved writerly sisters from the beginning. Holiday House gave me lifelong friends in Crystal and Joanne. And my debut group connected me to a community of gorgeously bookish souls. So much love to "golden girls" Megan, Cat, and Nancy, to "sprinters" and "MG loves" Sylvia, Alyssa, Nicole, Kaela, Caroline, Melissa, Erica, and Jen. Yvette and Alysa, I couldn't come up with a name big enough for what your friendship means to me.

And always, always, always, my family.

Thank you, Bub, Sarah, Kat, Gracie, Libby, and Hannah, for being such enthusiastic cheerleaders.

Thank you, Mom and Dad, for so many things that I'd need a whole book's worth of pages to list them. In lieu of that, this story is dedicated to you, with love.

Thank you, Luke and Olivia, for letting me read to you, both when you were little, and now that you're not. Thank you for story ideas (all credit where credit is due for overflowing toilets and glass eyes). Thank you for doing whatever is the opposite of complaining when I tell you I'll be disappearing with my laptop for a bit. Thank you for the bright, shining lights of your souls. You are my miracles.

And Matt. You're last for a reason. Because you're the be-all and end-all for me.